RESERVATION
NATION

RESERVATION

NATION

A NOVEL

DAVID FULLER COOK

BOAZ PUBLISHING COMPANY
Albany, California

Reservation Nation. Copyright © 2007 by David Fuller Cook. All rights reserved. No part of this book may be reproduced in any form or by any electronic or mechanical means, or the facilitation thereof, including information storage and retrieval systems, without permission in writing from the publisher, except by a reviewer, who may quote brief passages in a review. Address all inquiries to:
Boaz Publishing Company
968 Ordway Street
Albany, CA 94706.
www.boazpublishing.com

Cover photograph: Ken Tiger at Wounded Knee South Dakota, 1973, by Michelle Vignes. Courtesy of The Bancroft Library, University of California, Berkeley.
Edited by Robin Smith.
Cover and interior design by Elizabeth Vahlsing.
First Edition. Printed in the United States of America.

Library of Congress Cataloging-in-Publication Data
Cook, Dave F. (Dave Fuller), 1951-
    Reservation nation : a novel / David Fuller Cook. -- 1st ed.
        p. cm.
    Winner of the Fabri Literary Prize.
    ISBN 978-1-893448-04-9 (alk. paper)
1. Indian reservations--Fiction. 2. Indians of North America--
Fiction. 3. Domestic fiction. I. Title.

PS3603.O5688R47 2007
813'.6--dc22

                                                    2007031497

To my brother Sam;
and my sister Jo,
For your compassion
In all life's trials.

THIS WHICH FOLLOWS IS A WORK OF FICTION
AND DOES NOT PERTAIN TO THE DIRECT EXPERIENCE
OF ANY TRIBE OR THE REAL EXPERIENCE OF ANY
TRIBE'S MEMBERS. AS A CULTURAL IDENTITY THE
UWHARRIE PEOPLE PASSED FROM PHYSICAL EXISTENCE
IN THE 1700S. THE TRUTH OF THIS STORY IS
METAPHORICAL, AND IS INTENDED TO SPEAK TO THE
ISSUES OF POVERTY, ASSIMILATION, CULTURAL
SURVIVAL AND PROPHECY.

My name is Warren Eubanks, the Seed; I am Uwharrie. No one told me I was Uwharrie until I was eleven years old. I *thought* I was Indian but didn't know that being Indian was more than not being white, that truth is more than what's not a lie.

The main road on the Old Reservation was a dirt road called Reservation Road. It was one way in and one way out, a dead-end road. I lived near the top of that road with Grandmother and Grandfather in a house my grandfather built. If I hadn't've lived with them I would have been adopted or something, like my sister Ruby, or sent to Indian boarding school the way many kids were, because my mom and dad got killed in a car crash.

When I was a kid our fathers and mothers were not talking about continuing to be Indian and many of the old people weren't saying anything, and I guess mostly a lot of people were trying to figure out how *not* to be an Indian, and my father had been the chief of that. I didn't know until later the reason for the blue smoke around him. Back in the fifties there were some on the Reservation who were for termination. They were saying that if they had the deeds to the land they lived on, then they could improve their homes. They were fed up with being wards of the federal government and wanted to pay their taxes like everybody else so they could hold their heads up and look the world in the face. They said they didn't like it, Chief Billy dressing up in his furry head gear, like a Sioux or something, in a Christmas parade, but Chief Billy was always willing to do it, what he called furthering our interests and getting the white people to do things for us.

There was a lot of not-saying on the Reservation when I was a kid. I learned it. I had to unlearn it, because I knew there was something nobody was talking about. I could feel it. But I didn't know if it was true because I was a kid. I felt silence where words or laughing or crying were meant to be.

"That is your Owl medicine," Aunt Ida said to me. "You feel what nobody says, even to themselves. If they never say it they never know why they lived. You have known this immediately for a long time."

She meant that the knowledge came from the time of our ancestors, when we emerged as a distinct culture, as a people.

"I can't tell you much more than that," she said. "Women don't have to do anything special, if we stay off alcohol. We're pretty much accessible anyway, but in the old days young men would go off alone— no food, no water—and sit by themselves. Women don't have to do that. It's easier for us, but then, life is harder."

I don't think Aunt Ida would have told me this except, by this time, my father had gotten himself drunk and killed in a car crash, and maybe it was an accident and maybe it wasn't, but he wouldn't be asking me at supper, "What is this bullshit about an owl?"

There's a lot I don't remember about my mom, and memories I'll never have, but there was some kind of disagreement between my mom and my grandmother. I don't know what it was. Maybe it was because Mom didn't do much, or didn't try as hard as Grandmother wanted her to. Mom never took up the weaving, and it seemed like the only words shared between them were those they had to say.

"Your mother was a very strong woman, in her own way," Aunt Ida told me when I asked her about it. "Your mother just knew what to do."

Aunt Ida lived at the top of the mountain in the next to the last house on Reservation Road. Aunt Ida was my great aunt; even when I was a boy she was old. She tied her hair back in a cloud-white bun, had a sharp nose like a hawk, and eyes like a hawk too. She knew what you were doing all the time. She could read minds; she could read mine anyway. She had a particular way with dogs, another way with chickens, and another way with horses or cows. She had words in the old language that was a way of speaking with them, but I never got the chance to really learn them.

I remember when I was a kid, one day after school, we were pitching hay into the hay loft and Aunt Ida said to me, "Warren, the cow doesn't like you and Joe Bad Crow throwing rocks at her."

Sometimes Aunt Ida would chain the cow. I'm not sure why she did this, because mostly she let that old cow wander anywhere she liked. That cow never went far. She liked Aunt Ida. All the animals did. But one day Joe Bad Crow and I found out Aunt Ida had chained the cow and so we snuck up on her, like we were great hunters, and threw rocks at her, knowing she would chase us. But she had that chain around her neck. We knew she'd run out of chain. We thought we were being brave.

"How do you know we were throwing rocks at the cow?" I asked her. "Did you see us?"

"No."

"Who told you then?"

"She did," Aunt Ida said, still pitching hay. "She wanted me to ask you to stop throwing rocks at her."

That was all she said. The next time Aunt Ida chained the cow Joe was ready to head out to the field where that cow was and throw rocks at her but I told him what Aunt Ida had said.

"What does she know?" Joe said. But we didn't throw rocks at the cow anymore.

Aunt Ida said small birds were bright thoughts, said that if a person was having trouble with negative thoughts they could keep their eye out for small birds and that would help them: tanagers and redbirds, field buntings most people never notice, sparrows too, for their happy movements.

Sun Susie, Aunt Ida's niece, worked the early shift at the hospital. I think Sun Susie got her love of horses from Aunt Ida. Before she got married Sun Susie lived with Aunt Ida, and even after she got married she always helped with the chickens and cows, but what she really loved was horses. Sun Susie loved horses more than anyone I've ever known, and she believed one day that she would move away from the Reservation for good and it would be because one of her horses won at the races. One of her horses was going to win at Red Rock or Lansdale and then everything would just get better. Maybe that horse would even win the Kentucky Derby or something. It never happened though. She was all her life waiting for a winner. Usually there were four or five horses she'd have at one time, but none of them ever won anything. Sun Susie would get home from her job at the hospital, in the middle of the afternoon, watch a soap opera on her TV and then she'd be out working those horses until dark and then get up and do it again. Sun Susie just kept putting her money into horse feed and keeping care of them, paying some skinny white man to come over with his truck and trailer and haul one of her horses over to the Lansdale race track once a month and then haul the horse back.

Grandfather said there were a lot of horses in the old days. Sun Susie would have been happier then, not because of the horses really, but because she wouldn't have had that disease in her blood, the way she was sick with worry, like a lot of white people. Sun Susie wore her hair in a ponytail and smoked those cigarettes. Most of the time she looked worried, older than she was, smoking those cigarettes, drinking a cooler of coffee, and getting dark circles under her eyes. Sun Susie smoked Marlboros. I always thought it was because they had horses in their commercials but Sun Susie said she had been smoking since she was thirteen years old. Her face looked a little bit like a horse. She was pretty but her teeth were big. She was skinny too. Aunt Ida was all the time telling her she should eat more.

"You eat like a bird," she would say. "Eat up!"

Sun Susie might not eat another bite. She might get up from the table and stomp off. I could see it. I could see the blue smoke. It wasn't cigarette smoke; it was blue smoke. I didn't see it so clearly until after the yearling had gotten himself tangled up in the fence. That was a sad thing. Me and Grandfather had come every day to watch at the fence, watching where that young stallion ran up and down. He bucked and threw his head back and snorted at the sky like he was remembering the wild from where he came from. That young stallion was one fine-looking horse, had the heart of ten brave men. The pasture, the whole wide world was his. He was a dreamer and he was dreaming of when he would run the whole wide world.

"He's a winner," Grandfather had said. "This is the one Sun Susie has been waiting for. He will make her happy and win many races."

But that young stallion ran into the barbed wire fence. He must have been running fast because he tore himself up bad. Maybe he was trying to get out. He broke one of the strands of barbed wire and got his leg tangled up. He was ripped up pretty bad because Sun Susie sent for the vet, and horse doctors cost money. It was worse than they thought, tore tendons or something, and that young horse didn't become the champion he was born to be.

"The world is different now," Grandfather said. "Sometimes things don't happen the way they're supposed to. There didn't used to be any metal to keep horses from running where they were born to run. There was never supposed to be a barbed wire fence there, and that's why he couldn't see it."

"But isn't that just the universe balancing itself out?" I said, because this was something Grandfather was teaching me.

"I don't know," he said. "That horse is a winner; it's just that he's never going to do it at the big-time race track with all the white men with the money come to watch."

Grandfather told Aunt Ida that Sun Susie should get rid of her horses.

"They're not happy," Grandfather said. "If they were happy they would win all the time. If those horses were happy there wouldn't be one white man's horse that could beat them. How can they be happy with a fence such as the Kowache have?"

"If there wasn't that fence those horses would leave," Aunt Ida said. "Gordon Gannon would probably catch them and say they were his." It was her way of keeping Grandfather from saying anymore about Sun Susie's horses. She just wanted Sun Susie to be happy.

Like many on the Reservation, Sun Susie was caught up in forces she didn't understand. Maybe you could say Sun Susie's father's drinking split up her family but that doesn't say where he got it from; it had all the symptoms of the Kowache disease, the spirit sickness. She sure did love horses though. In Sun Susie's family there was a tension between the old ways—the words and the stories—and Presbyterianism and the white ways. There were family silences, things unsaid, which broke out in twisted ways, as arguments, bad words and thoughts. Sun Susie's two brothers grew up in foster homes, and when Sun Susie was in her teens she ran away from her foster home, hitchhiked to Utah, lived with a cousin or something and eventually moved to California. A couple of years later she phoned Aunt Ida, and Aunt Ida bought her a bus ticket home from San Jose. Sun Susie moved back to the Reservation, moved in with Aunt Ida. Maybe Sun Susie had an innate attraction to suffering and that's why she got killed the way she did, buried somewhere over behind Old Man's Back. It isn't directly understood because white people were involved.

What I was taught—and they taught it in church and school—was that if you couldn't be white—which you couldn't—you had to learn how to get along in the Kowache world, to live in white man's time. Mostly it was done by way of language, history and geography. They'd wash your mouth out with soap in the Reservation School if you said one word in the Uwharrie language, and there was no word of our stories. In the Reservation School they took away our words, replaced them with English and taught us that we were a mistaken people: the last of our native speakers were dying. With them were dying the words which made us who we are.

According to Mr. Brown, and he was the teacher at the Reservation School and a Presbyterian too, Indians lived the way we did because we didn't know any better.

Mr. Brown plastered his hair down with oil so it looked like he was wearing a cap, had a long neck and was always thapping a ruler in his hand. He was the one who taught us in the Reservation School not to ask for anything, not for anything at all, not even a drink of water. I mean you're a kid and it's time for you to go to the bathroom, except you can't because you have to wait until somebody else tells you it's time to go to the bathroom. That kind of stuff messes with your mind.

"Your fathers and grandfathers didn't know the

great potential the land has for growing crops," Mr. Brown would say. "The machinery now available to us means we can farm more land, and improve land your grandfathers didn't think was farmable. Indians didn't know what to do with the land. They just lived on it."

Ruay Overmoon always enjoyed saying to me that going to the Reservation School could make me stupid like a white child, that Kowache children just get more stupid, until by the time they are grown up they are ignorant as hell. Grandmother didn't like me going to the Reservation School. Hell, *I* didn't like going to the Reservation School, but there wasn't anything either of us could do about it.

Grandmother was always giving me things; I didn't know it. She gave me my love of the woods, the flowers of the Earth. I look at the white-pink sprigs of mountain laurel with their dark green leaves in the mist after a thunderstorm and I think of her.

Whenever Grandmother was working, cleaning or shelling beans or whatever, she sang the old songs, especially when she was weaving, sitting on the rug by the east window in the sun. Grandmother did her weaving in the morning. The loom was off the rug right next to the window, but at an angle so the sunlight came in and shined on Grandmother. When she worked in the kitchen she hunched over the table or the sink, but when she was working at her loom, she looked like she had an oak board stuck right up her back. It was the only time I remember her sitting very straight. A year before she died though, she couldn't do any weaving because her back hurt so much, her hands too. Arthritis bothered her fingers, particularly in the mornings, so sometimes she couldn't weave. She'd get mean and cranky if she couldn't weave.

When Grandmother was dying she said things to me like, "Warren, take that basket over there on the table. Your great aunt Mary Bright Bird made that basket. I don't need it anymore. You should have it." It was a traditional basket with that spiral woven in.

She'd point all over that room, "Warren, you see that photograph of your great grandfather? That was taken by a white-man anthropologist on his way to Mexico. He mailed it back here. You should keep it."

"You see that piece of windwood? You see that rug lying over there? You see that pottery jug on the shelf? Your Aunt Beebee made that. You should have it."

Grandmother gave all her stuff away before she died. If you didn't take what she gave you, it might not be there when you came back. Grandmother gave Janey Morning Cloud the wicker chair she was sitting in one day. My grandmother was in bed, and pointed to it and said, "Janey, you should have that." Well, Janey Morning Cloud didn't take it right away, and when she came back Grandmother was sleeping and Janey said to me, "Where's my chair? It was sitting right here."

I had to tell her, "Oh. Grandmother gave that chair away a couple of days ago."

Janey Morning Cloud fussed and fumed some, but what could she do? Grandmother had given her chair away, that's all.

I learned pretty quick if I wanted something I better take it. But people who came in just every once in awhile, brought some cookies or something, if Grandmother gave them something, they might not know to take it while they had it. "Oh, we'll come back and get that sometime, Margaret," they'd say.

But when they came back with more cookies that thing might be gone. Grandmother was a very generous person. When she knew she wasn't going to get up out of that bed, she couldn't give her stuff away fast enough, and I mean everything down to a flat stone she had picked or a turtle shell she'd laid by on a shelf. One day I'm looking at a piece of uranium ore she had on a shelf. She didn't know what it was, but I knew what it was because I had been down there at the Legion Hall when two government geologists had been passing around samples of pitchblende and uranite. I knew what uranium looked like and how heavy it felt when you held it in your hand, and that day she saw me looking at it and said, "Warren, what you looking at?"

"Oh nothing. Just this piece of uranium you got. Grandmother, where did you get this uranium?"

"Uranium? Is that what it is? Oh yeah, I think maybe your grandfather gave that to me," she said. "I don't know where I got it, but Warren, you like rocks, you should have it."

I didn't have much use for it but I kept it, because Grandmother wanted me to.

Reverend Blake came to visit Grandmother before she died. She wasn't a convert. I think he was expecting he'd be coming back again to give Grandmother her last rites and all, but Grandmother wouldn't have it. It never happened.

Reverend Blake was a pink-faced puffy man. He wasn't stern but he was relentless, wear you down with kindness and tell you why things were the way they were, and how God meant them that way, how if there was something bad going on there was a good reason for it. According to Reverend Blake, civilizing the Indian was an act of great mercy; we were our own fault and he could explain the rich and the poor, and the white way over all the creatures of the Earth, including the Indian, as corresponding to the will of God, and all the time calling us children. When Reverend Blake started in on one of his sermons, he'd straighten out his arms and hold on to that pulpit like he was riding a tractor, and smile at us with that pink face of his, taking deep breaths, like he was filling up with the holy spirit. That's what he called it. The sermons were really the best part of going to church because you didn't have to pay attention. You didn't have to stand up and repeat whatever Reverend Blake was saying, or sing from the hymn book, or kneel on the benches of grainy wood that left notches in your knees. When Reverend Blake went into his sermon, I'd look up at the sun stream-

ing through the church windows, maybe I'd hear a
wren singing, and I would pass into a reverie, a med-
itation. Those were sacred moments. I knew
Reverend Blake meant well, but that kind of truth
doesn't take that long to tell.

Dr. Stevenson plied Grandmother with his medicine too, but she wouldn't have any more to do with
his medicine than she would Reverend Blake's reli-
gion. He was full-time at the Presbyterian Hospital,
but before the government built the Infirmary, Dr.
Stevenson would come around about once a month
and pass out medicine from out of the back of his
blue Plymouth: tins of salve, liniment, quinine,
strychnine, all sorts of shit. He was an angular man,
all angles, so even his glasses wouldn't fit on his face.
The smoke around him was kind of a pukey green-
grey. He'd drive up in a cloud of dust and there'd be
ten or fifteen people waiting for him. Sun Susie
would help him give out the medicine and he'd pay
her off in cigarettes, and later on, after she went to
the community college, helped her get a job at the
hospital. Dr. Stevenson was the one who sewed people up when they got into fights, but you didn't get
away just getting sewn up because he was some kind
of deacon or something and was the one who came
after you if you weren't in church. We were forced to
go to school and we were forced to go to church. If
you missed a Sunday Dr. Stevenson or some other
Presbyterian would come around on Monday to find
out what was wrong with you. The thing about it was

I could tell Dr. Stevenson wasn't blessed or happy. He had the white man's disease, or maybe you'd just call him a hard man. There were his words and then there was who he was.

"Never look a Presbyterian in the eye," Ruay Overmoon used to like to say.

"Why is that?" I would ask him.

"Because they will want to talk to you."

That seemed like a strange thing for *him* to say because you had to be careful when you talked to Ruay Overmoon; he could keep you for hours and you might miss dinner.

Even Gary Yellow Knife talked about how sinful Indians were and how bad we were, like we were the cause of our own suffering and that's why things were the way they were. Gary Yellow Knife was really big into that stuff and his talk was full of spirits who were happy, and other spirits who would suffer for all time, Indians whose spirits would drift around forever with no place to land because of what they'd done. It didn't sound all that different from what Reverend Blake and Dr. Stevenson were saying, but kinder somehow.

"Oh, *you* don't have anything to worry about, Margaret," Gary Yellow Knife said to Grandmother before she died. He was dressed in his bone shirt, his leggings and his moccasins that his granddaughter, Ruth Upchurch, had made for him, and so Grandmother felt better, more at peace anyway, because she did suffer some before she died.

When Grandmother died Grandfather stopped talking. For more than a month he didn't say a word to anyone, not even to Ruay Overmoon.

One day in the garden me and Grandfather were picking beans and I said to him, "Grandfather, are you ever going to talk again?"

He looked at me, and I thought he was just going to go back to picking more beans when he said, "Warren, there aren't words for everything. And I don't have much to say right now, but if I think of something you'll be the first to know."

Grandfather started doing that thing he called "balancing the universe." It had a lot of implications and might even have to do with why it wasn't raining or why Macy Ryden was all the time having baby girls when Tut Ryden wanted a son. It had to do with the future and the past, in accordance with the old ways, which Grandfather and Ruay Overmoon knew as well as anybody, how the victory of the Kowache over the Uwharrie never had to have happened. We weren't supposed to be living on the Reservation except the old ones hadn't balanced the universe, when it was the time to do that.

My sister Ruby and Sun Susie thought Grandfather was acting crazy when Grandmother died, but I knew what he was doing. He moved Grandmother's loom to Aunt Ida's house and bought a TV and put it where Grandmother's loom used to be. We didn't even have electricity. I came home from work one day and he was sitting there on the floor, on that rug where Grandmother used to sit, watching a grey TV screen.

"Grandfather," I said, "we don't have electricity. Those things need electricity."

"I know."

"Well, what are you going to do with that thing?" I said.

"I'm doing it."

"But what are you doing?"

"I'm balancing the universe."

It could get kind of complicated. The way Ruay Overmoon put it, "Usually when you fix one thing you have to fix another." Kind of like if you jack up a house on one side to make the kitchen level it puts a strain on the timbers in the living room and the plaster cracks. "It's better to let the big wind blow over before you set in to fix the house," he said.

I knew things were better when Grandfather started going down to Sun Susie's house every afternoon to watch the soap operas before Sun Susie went off to feed the horses. Sun Susie had a TV and electricity and got off work at the hospital at three o'clock. If I went over there they might be sitting on the porch talking about soap operas. Sun Susie would be smoking those cigarettes; she smoked like a chimney.

Grandfather loved to watch gangster movies and Westerns. I'd go over there in the evening with him and watch the gangster movies and the Westerns with him. There was one Indian, I can't remember his name, but he'd play an Italian, a Mafia type, because he could pass for Italian. And there was this one movie grandfather liked a lot because this Indian would kneel by a safe and break the code by listening to the tumblers fall into place. Grandfather could have watched that all day long. "This is the movie where the Indian breaks into the safe," he'd cackle, and he'd be delighted just to watch that whole movie for that one part, because it wasn't a very big part. The Indian breaks into the safe and he gets shot in the getaway.

Grandfather watched the Westerns because he liked to pick out the Indians and how many times you'd see the same Indian again, getting shot off his horse.

"Look there," Grandfather would say. "That's William Eagleshirt. That's the third time he's gotten shot off his horse!"

"Who's William Eagleshirt?" I would say. "Is he Uwharrie?"

"No," Grandfather would say, "but I met him once."

I didn't ever say anything, because Grandfather had never been off the Reservation that I knew of, so I don't see how he could have ever met William Eagleshirt or anybody else who was on TV.

Chief Billy Farmer sold the mineral rights on the Seven Mountains to the Kowache, and Sun Susie took a fancy to Jimmy Bird, who had left the Reservation for awhile to drive gasoline trucks out in Arizona on the Navaho Reservation. He looked like an ax, lean and hard, a shock of black hair greased with Vaseline, and when he was splitting wood and came across a knot, Jimmy Bird went through it.

The Big Cypress wells reopened because a new oil boom was on. White people wanted their gasoline, but nobody here seemed to be seeing any money, though some people had jobs. Good and bad can come to the same thing, because belief is only half the truth. When oil got discovered in the Kachawna Basin and some money started coming in, people had a hard time with it. Families got an initial check for five hundred dollars that first year and two hundred dollars each year in 1955 and 1956. There were all kinds of salesmen selling stuff on the Reservation and you might see two brand-new automobiles right beside a cinder-block house. There were brand-new electric washing machines, refrigerators, toasters and stuff sitting on the porches and yards of Uwharrie families because they didn't have any electricity. Yeah, salesmen were having a field day. Chief Billy said oil was helping our people and some could believe it, but oil wasn't as good a thing as everybody said. The problem was there was a lot of suffering on the

Reservation: alcoholism, no jobs, depression, suicide—maybe even more than when there wasn't oil being pumped out of the Reservation. Maybe the oil didn't cause this; maybe you couldn't just say it was white people who made this happen. Maybe it was a spiritual sickness. They were the ones who said oil was going to help us, but we were the ones who believed it.

Jimmy Bird moved back and made good money making runs north to Noble's Fork where the gasoline was loaded onto a train. Still, he'd be gone for a week at a time.

I'd hear Jimmy Bird start his truck in the dark of a Monday morning and lay awake waiting for him to pull down from the end of the Reservation Road and roll by our house. This was before Sun Susie and Jimmy Bird were married. In those days he'd come home early on Fridays, very happy and joking with everybody. He was a lot of fun back then, laughed and even played games with the children. I don't know if he was drinking in those days or not, when he and Sun Susie began going out together. Later, after Grandmother died, I'm sure he was drinking.

Grandmother never liked Jimmy Bird. She called him a "no-good" and said that if Sun Susie married him she'd be sorry. I knew somehow that what she said was true but I didn't want to hear it. I liked walking by the barn and smelling that big truck of his. It smelled like wood and oil and gasoline. It was red, the paint faded by hard work and sun, almost pink.

Jimmy Bird's big truck was too big for the upper part of the road, and Grandfather got angry with him for bringing that big old truck down such a little dirt road where he parked it down below Aunt Ida's barn. Grandfather said Jimmy Bird was tearing up the road.

Grandmother was right about Jimmy Bird, but I liked Jimmy Bird. He used to come over with his chain saw and cut firewood for Grandfather. I wouldn't look at why he was doing that. That sure made our life easier, but for some reason Grandmother said she didn't want Jimmy Bird cutting firewood for us. Maybe Jimmy Bird had started drinking by then, or maybe he'd started beating Sun Susie; I don't know. I can remember Sun Susie's face bruised and her smoking cigarettes, complaining how the races were fixed.

There was good in Jimmy Bird, but there was bad in him too, and there always seemed to be a fight between the two, even when he was smiling. Some Kowache man in town shot his own dog because the dog had done something he didn't like, and he shot that dog and left him on the street to suffer and die. Jimmy Bird was there. He didn't see that happen but he was in town and he heard about it; the dog was crying and dragging his hindquarters trying to get himself home. Jimmy Bird got a gun out of his truck and went and finished the job. He shot the dog. He put the dog in a burlap sack and went to the man's house and knocked on the door. When that white man came to the door Jimmy Bird said, "Here's your dog you left dying. If anything like that happens again it'll be you in this bag!" and he flung that bag into the man's house and walked away.

Indians didn't do that kind of thing, but Jimmy Bird did, and that white man never messed with him. Nobody did. He had red smoke around him, and maybe the white people thought he was crazy.

When Jimmy Bird and Sun Susie got married Aunt Ida wanted to give them a really big present. She had a black Studebaker and she loaded stuff into that Studebaker you'd never think of hauling in a car. She hauled chickens around in that car, and a goat more than once. One Christmas I was helping her move a bunch of Sun Susie's stuff, so that car was already full when Aunt Ida said she wanted to drive into town and pick up a woodstove as a wedding present for Sun Susie and Jimmy Bird. I don't know what got into her. It wasn't like her to want anything so bad as she wanted to get that woodstove into the backseat of her Studebaker, but for awhile Sun Susie seemed happy and that made Aunt Ida happy.

"Don't you think we should unload this other stuff first, Aunt Ida?" I said.

"Nah, there'll be room," she said.

Well, there wasn't. There wasn't room for that woodstove, much less all that other stuff too: chairs and lamps, suitcases, a basket of clothes, three or four boxes of dishes, and some grocery bags full of stuff Sun Susie had thrown together at the last minute. It had started snowing and what I didn't know was that Aunt Ida had already paid for the woodstove and gotten the white man at the hardware store to leave it on the sidewalk because he was closing at five o'clock, no matter what. And though that woodstove was too heavy for her to load by herself, he sure wasn't going to help her load it. He was a white man and she was an Indian. We got there in the dark, about five-thirty or six o'clock. There was already two inches of snow on top of that woodstove. A pretty big snowstorm was coming in from off the mountains. First we had to take all that stuff out of the car. It was a two-door Studebaker so we tried wedging that huge woodstove in behind the front seat but it was too big and we ripped more of the cloth upholstery trying to do it.

"It's not going to fit," I said.

"It'll fit," Aunt Ida said.

Then Aunt Ida got the idea to take out the front seat. We had all that stuff in the street, and the front seat too, and the snow falling fast. There was four inches of snow on the sidewalk and the stove still didn't fit. Then Aunt Ida got the idea of taking off the car door. That wasn't easy except that Aunt Ida had done it before. So we took the car door off on the rider's side, because you sure couldn't fit that woodstove in by the steering wheel. The car door was in the street, the front seat, and all that other stuff, when we finally got that woodstove into the backseat of Aunt Ida's Studebaker.

We loaded up a bunch of that stuff in the back-seat, stuffing it in around and on top of the wood-stove. Then we put the front seat back in, put the car door back on, and loaded up all the rest of the stuff that we had in the street.

"There's no room for me," I said when we finished loading. There was probably six or seven inches of snow on the ground by then and the wind was starting to blow hard.

"You'll fit," Aunt Ida said.

Well, there sure wasn't room in the front seat so I squeezed myself in through some chair legs and between some grocery bags. What I didn't know was Aunt Ida didn't want Sun Susie or Jimmy Bird to know what she had bought for them for Christmas and as a wedding present. That woodstove, that was a really big gift. Aunt Ida had decided we were going to unload that woodstove while Sun Susie and Jimmy Bird were off buying more stuff or getting blood tests or something.

Aunt Ida had to drive down behind the barn, across the cattle guard, down through a pasture, across a wooden bridge and up the hill pasture on the other side until she got to the little house Sun Susie and Jimmy Bird were moving into. Most times she could have done that. The only trouble was there was more than a foot of snow on the ground and it was dark. She couldn't see the bridge at all because the creek and the streambed were filled up with snow. What was worse, by the time I realized what was happening Aunt Ida was already rolling downhill toward the creek. She really wanted that woodstove to be a surprise.

"Hold on!" she cried out.

I knew we were in trouble when she said that, because she couldn't see where the bridge was. Aunt Ida was just going to guess where it was. We picked up speed because you had to have enough speed to make it up the hill on the other side in the deep snow, so Aunt Ida gunned it right before we got to the creek. I knew when I felt a thump underneath the floorboard that we weren't going to make it. Half the car was on the bridge but the other half wasn't. The good thing was we didn't flip because of the snow being so deep, or because we hit the bank on the other side.

I was alright because I was packed in there tight with the chairs and the grocery bags, but Aunt Ida got a gash on her forehead which bled pretty bad. I saw the blood in the snow the next day when Chief Billy pulled the car out with his tractor. He was the only one who had a tractor. Aunt Ida was holding her hand on her head and she had still wanted to unload all that stuff that night, carry it in the dark and the deep snow about fifty yards. Mostly she wanted to get that woodstove in there so it could be a surprise for Sun Susie and Jimmy Bird. It was so stupid that we finally gave it up.

As it turned out Sun Susie and Jimmy Bird weren't coming back that night anyway. They had never planned on coming back that night, because the snow was so deep and the house didn't have any heat anyway. They didn't know about that woodstove or that Aunt Ida had had Grandfather cut some wood for them that afternoon. It had all been Aunt Ida's idea, how, after we got that stuff unloaded, and the woodstove fitted and piped, she was going to go home, where Sun Susie and Jimmy Bird were staying until the house was ready, and say, "Your house is ready for you. Get your stuff and come on."

And Jimmy Bird was going to say, "No, it's not ready. There's no heat in that house."

And then Aunt Ida was going to say, with a big smile, "Oh yes there is. Come on, come see." That's what she'd wanted all along. She was really happy about it all.

But it didn't turn out the way she wanted it to, and later she admitted that her wanting had been dust in her eyes. The snow piled up and we got twenty inches before it was over. It was five or six days before Sun Susie and Jimmy Bird moved in, and they knew about the woodstove long before that. They helped take the front door off and pull the front seat out again to get that woodstove unloaded. It was one big woodstove. It heated the whole house.

I guess we knew Jimmy Bird was beating Sun Susie. I'd known it for awhile, and I knew he wasn't going to stay and that she would have to ask him to leave, because of the horses, and because he didn't really love her. She would never be able to tell herself that, but I knew she would say something to him anyway, but the words wouldn't come out right exactly. She wouldn't say, "Jimmy, you don't really love me." She would say something about how she couldn't live that way, that she was too unhappy. Jimmy Bird would say something about her always being unhappy.

I don't know if Jimmy Bird started beating Sun Susie because of the drink, or if that's the way he really was. I asked Aunt Ida how Sun Susie got such bruises on her face, and she told me Sun Susie had fallen off her horse and that was how she got those bruises. But I knew she couldn't be falling off her horse that much. I think Aunt Ida liked Jimmy Bird too, and was hoping things weren't happening the way they were, or that they would get better. Sun Susie was smoking three or four packs of cigarettes a day then. She'd be hanging halters in the barn, carrying bucket after bucket of water and feed, forking hay, and all the time a cigarette in her mouth and those purple bruises on her face. She was pretty but with those bruises on her face she looked unhappy. Nobody looks pretty when they're unhappy, no matter how pretty they are.

One day people stopped believing in Jimmy Bird. It didn't happen all at once, but one night Jimmy was driving north out of the Reservation on State Road 57, making a run to Noble's Fork, and got pulled over by an inspector, who had figured out that the new pipelines could carry all the oil produced on the Reservation, meaning that few, if any, trucks needed to be hauling oil from the oil wells. Jimmy Bird didn't have a run ticket, what he needed to show it was okay to be hauling oil off of the Reservation.

Jimmy Bird just kind of up and disappeared for awhile after that. He would show up from time to time, but it was never for long and nothing good ever happened from it. He'd ask Sun Susie for the money she was making at the hospital and beat her when she didn't give it to him. He'd tell her she was just selfish for spending all her money on those horses. He told Sun Susie she should stop believing that one of her horses was going to win that big race one day.

Sun Susie never did move back in with Aunt Ida, but kept living in her own house by herself, was living in that house the day she disappeared. It must have been a couple weeks after she disappeared that I went over to Aunt Ida's house and heard her grieving, not crying, but sheer wailing. I didn't know at that time that Sun Susie was dead for sure, thought maybe she'd gone off to California again, but when I heard Aunt Ida wailing like she was, I knew it wasn't just that Sun Susie had gone off to California. There were several women in the house that day when Aunt Ida was grieving like she was: Pearl Nanibush, Ruth Upchurch, Ruth Goins, maybe some others. I saw in through the window. Aunt Ida didn't say more than a couple of words for about six months.

Jimmy Bird wasn't the only one who got pulled over on State Road 57 for not having a run ticket. He was just the first. An investigative reporter came out with an article in *The Round Mountain Journal* estimating that thirty percent of Indian oil had been stolen since the oil fields opened in the mid-fifties. He thought the tribe should have been suspicious because oil prices had gone up from eight dollars a barrel to twenty-eight dollars a barrel in four years, but the tribe's royalties had only gone up twenty percent.

Chief Billy and the Tribal Council were skeptical that the problem was widespread, even though the newspaper article said there were more than just a few oil tankers leaving the Reservation. The article cited Uncle Sam Petroleum in particular, and at first it looked like there were going to be a whole bunch of convictions, but nothing ever happened with that. It was that way with oil, and Jimmy Bird never was officially stricken from the tribal register.

It turned out the tribe didn't have any real records of how much oil was coming out of the ground. That was the whole problem; U.S. Petroleum was self-regulating. It was stealing from itself. At that time there weren't any seals on the valves; oil wasn't measured at the wellhead but at the point of sale, and truckers could just pull up at a valve and start pumping. I guess that was what Jimmy Bird was doing, but I know it wasn't the kind of thing he was going to think up for himself. Somebody had to be paying him. Where are you going to take a truckload of oil?

Nobody in the tribe knew how much oil was coming out of the ground, and U.S. Petroleum were the ones saying how much oil was arriving at the treatment facilities and the storage tanks where the oil was sold, and then they'd lower the value of the oil by saying it had impurities in it, water and sediment, calling it waste oil. Federal regulations were supposed to prohibit good oil from being stored in spill ponds because it could be taken from spill ponds without passing through a meter.

It didn't matter that Uncle Sam Petroleum had mysteriously acquired and sold a lot of crude oil. That's what they said it was, maintained that they got it right out of junk-oil pits.

Chief Billy put on a good show and kept saying how "we are going to get to the bottom of this." U.S. Petroleum kept its lease and only a few people got convicted: a contract pumper and two truckers. There were a lot of people who thought Chief Billy knew about all this. Chief Billy was definitely one political Indian. When he got wind of what people were saying—that he knew about it all along—he held a tribal meeting, saying he wanted to be open and above board about what was going on with "the oil scandal." That's what he called it.

It was all Indians that night. It was down at the Legion Hall and Chief Billy started out saying how concerned he was, and that the problems in the oil industry weren't just a Uwharrie concern, but something for all tribes who had oil on their land to be concerned about. I don't how he got a copy of the *Denver Post*, but that night he read from an article in that paper saying that six percent of all the oil in the U.S. was stolen from reservation lands.

He talked a lot about USGS regulations and read from a report from the BIA, the Bureau of Indian Affairs, and said how we didn't want to pay out any tribal dollars and give somebody a job being an oil-field inspector when the federal government should pay for it. His big thing that night was how they were going to put numbered seals on all the meters—custody transfer meters—which would automatically measure the sale and couldn't be tampered with without somebody knowing it.

Hanay Rose stood up and said that was all well and good but who was going to make sure the valves were sealed.

Chief Billy's idea was that the oil-field inspectors would know that, but there wasn't one oil-field inspector at the meeting—there were only three of them all together—so Chief Billy could see his way to pretty much saying whatever he wanted to.

We got numbered seals on all the meters, and the promise that Chief Billy would look into getting more inspectors.

Jimmy Bird just kind of up and disappeared, and the tribal police didn't go after him as far as I know. It was a matter that had to do with oil and that's the way it was. It wasn't long before he was a story, living in North Dakota, driving a truck for the Sioux, and when Sun Susie disappeared some people thought maybe Jimmy Bird had something to do with it. We were wrong about that but it would be many years before we would really know.

My sister, Ruby Keehoe, moved back to the Reservation a couple of years after she dropped out of college in Utah in 1961, and Sun Susie helped her get a job at the Presbyterian Hospital. Ruby was five years older than me, so I really didn't know her until after she moved back to the Reservation. When she first came back to the Reservation Ruby was knock-dead gorgeous, not like out of a magazine; it wasn't that kind of beauty. You couldn't say, "Oh, she looks like Marilyn Monroe or Jane Russell"; she was big-boned, and before she gained some weight, pretty good-looking. Even then she was pretty, maybe because of those big bones she had. She didn't look like anybody else.

Ruby had been raised Mormon, so when she moved back to the Reservation, I studied on the *Book of Mormon* for awhile, because she was big into that. There's something in it but I couldn't altogether figure it out. Thomas Matoas Paint said he saw some sense in that book, because the past and the future are embedded in the present moment—like how the prophesies, for Mormons, were written down on gold plates but not dug up until the 1800s because that's when they were supposed to get dug up, but they were written before Jesus was born. Thomas liked that story. He said it made sense. It never made sense to me.

Ruby had wanted to help people, become a lawyer, or it was Grandfather who wanted her to help people, become a lawyer. I don't know where he got that idea but when she was living in Utah she was all the time wanting to come back to the Reservation, find out who she was. But then, whenever Grandfather got Sun Susie to write a letter for him, he would tell her to stay away: "Go to school! Go to school and then come back and help." Grandfather always knew she was coming back, even when Ruby didn't know it herself. I was too young at the time to know how that got decided, but from listening to Ruay Overmoon I know Grandmother wasn't for it, Ruby getting adopted and going to learn the ways of the white people from the inside out. Ruby told me later there were many nights when she cried. She wanted to be here.

She told me she loved her foster mother and father, and her two foster sisters and brother, and cried when she went away to college because she missed them too. She went to Brigham Young University for awhile, and lived afterwards in Utah for a short while because she met a young man in college and thought they might get married. That didn't work out and she moved back to the Reservation, and got that job at the hospital hoping to save up enough money for law school. But Grandmother had died by that time, and there were some things Ruby couldn't make sense of; Grandfather couldn't tell her any women's wisdom. She talked to Aunt Ida a lot, and then Ruby got married to Joe Bad Crow and they had two sons, Jason and Anthony John. Maybe it was because of all that happened with Joe Bad

Crow, but Ruby never did go to law school. It didn't work out that way.

Joe Bad Crow and Ruby were as different as the sun and the moon. They loved each other and they hated each other. When they had two sons, they were different too, like fire and water. Anthony John grew up and built houses for people, white people, for money, and on the Reservation too. Jason just kind of drowned himself in the water of life.

It couldn't have been easy being Joe's son. He wasn't easy to understand because he was all mixed in white man's time. Joe Bad Crow would have made a fine warrior in the old days, and sometimes I think he was mad because he'd been born too late for the old days. As hot tempered as he was, Joe had a warrior's mind and saw things in the brink of the moment, something most people can't do.

There was the time Joe drowned two German shepherds out in the oil fields in an evaporating pond. He had a job for awhile as an inspector in the oil fields. This was before they had regulations about petroleum pits and ponds. You didn't have to have a cover on an evaporation pond in those days. In fact, I don't think you can even have an evaporation pond these days, because the government changed all that. Used to be you just opened a valve and the separated water ran off to the nearest ditch or into a pond. That was some nasty water and there started to be regulations about that, but even so, we had water running off into freshwater streams—and evaporation ponds—well into the sixties. Water was routed through a string of pits with baffles and skimmers to the pond, but a lot of that water leaving those pits seeped through the bottom instead of evaporating into the air. We had people getting sick and I think it was because of those pits and evaporation ponds.

One night Joe Bad Crow was walking around the evaporation ponds, supposed to carry a gun but all he ever carried with him was an old Bowie knife he'd found at the dump. This van drives up and these white guys get out. They've got dogs with them, two German shepherd attack dogs. These white guys let those dogs go and Joe started running up through the evaporation ponds. He knew there was no way he could outrun those dogs, and for all he knew they were going to kill him, so when he'd run far enough up along those evaporation ponds Joe waded into the water, about waist deep, and pulled off his shoes and shirt. One dog was faster than the other and jumped into the water after him. When that dog swam out to get him, Joe grabbed his head and held him down underwater, drowned him. The dog couldn't get his feet on the bottom. The other dog didn't figure it out and jumped in after the first dog, and Joe grabbed that dog and drowned him too. After that Joe cut across the hills, didn't even go back for his truck until the next day.

Joe felt bad about those dogs. Those dogs were just doing what they'd been trained to do, but when Joe told Ruby about it she got all pissed off because he had drowned two dogs. She loved dogs.

After Jason died, died in Arizona from a drug overdose, it was like there was a valley of darkness between Joe and Ruby no words could cross. Ruby went moody and Joe just started drinking.

Jason must have hitchhiked across the United States nine or ten times. We kept hoping something would hold Jason on the Reservation, but he'd stay with Ruby a couple of days and then he'd be gone again. Then one day he'd walk in through the door just like we had just seen him yesterday. We'd drink a beer and he'd tell his stories: the time he'd almost gotten killed by Cubans sitting outside a hotel in Miami; some guys in Arizona going to rape him but he got out of the car by kicking one guy in the teeth; two soldiers in Florida picking him up on an Everglades highway and going 130 miles an hour, weaving in and out of traffic, and the driver looking back at Jason saying, "How you like this ride, Injun?" Joe couldn't stand those stories, and it always ended up with him getting mad and telling Jason how stupid he was, but Jason just kind of walked in the white man's world but just couldn't believe in it. Maybe he was one of the old ones.

I think when Jason was a kid he saw his world coming apart. You could see that in his eyes. There's something to a husband and a wife fighting that injures a child's spirit, hurts them where it can't be seen. It works on their faith, erodes their belief that things can work out in this world. I'm pretty sure Joe felt guilty about what happened to Jason; I know I did. Yet guilt, doubt, worry, hope, regret, self-pity, comparison: these are thoughts, thoughts the white man brought us. There never was a word "free," nothing to free ourselves from, until the Kowache came. It was all here, inside the circle.

After Jason died Ruby got interested in the history of our people in a way she never had before. The stories. It was like she was all the time trying to make up for it, the sadness. She wasn't going to miss a powwow or a Feast Day, and she wasn't going to say no to anybody's fry bread or miss a corn cake. She was still pretty, maybe because of those big bones she had, but it was like she was making up for lost time—except nobody can make up for lost time. Out of that grief came some kind of sense of how the world had once been whole and that it wasn't quite that way anymore. It was almost like she was trying to be more Uwharrie than anybody. She wanted it so bad. It can't be put into words, the kind of belonging she hadn't found among the Kowache. They didn't know of it. It's language in the blood, deep in us, like the water of life—the river.

Sometimes after dinner, Ruby would walk down to the river just to look at it. She'd go down there by herself and smoke a cigarette. That's where I'd find her, but she didn't seem to want to talk about whatever it was that was making her heavyhearted, going down there way after dark just to hear the low slow flow of the water.

"Me and Joe don't agree on much," she'd say.

"But you sure do love each other," I'd say, and she'd look at me, look right through me, like she was trying to find out if I was lying. There would come a day when she would say, "Being poor is nothing to be proud of."

She'd tell me about those things that had happened to her, about what she knew about why she got adopted and the things which had changed her life, and how she had a feeling it was never going to work out between her and Joe. Then Ruby would start talking about how life was going downhill, that something was going wrong, and how this wasn't the way life was supposed to be.

I remember the morning in 1970 Joe Bad Crow told me he'd gotten drafted. He'd bought a six-pack of Budweiser and a bag of peanuts at the Poison Creek Store down off Highway 10. The Poison Creek Store was its own story. The Poison Creek Store down off Highway 10 got sold to Gordon Gannon who decided to call it the Wilson Creek Store. The Kowache called the creek running under Highway 10 Wilson Creek because a family named Wilson had lived on it, had had that land around that creek. That's the name that's on the maps too, Wilson Creek, but the way Joseph Calaitl tells it, everybody knew the Kowache were going to take that land. That creek was in the prophecy tales and Joseph Calaitl knew a lot of those stories.

"The old ones said it would happen," he said. What nobody knew was how it was going to happen. "That creek was first called Tulahwassi. *Tulah* means forked, like the tongue of a titmouse, because there are two big forks to that creek. But it was already known that the Kowache would get that land by means of betrayal. Everybody thought it would be a broken treaty. The Kowache had broken so many treaties it just seemed like that's what they would do again. But the Wilsons didn't break a treaty to get what they wanted.

"There were Uwharrie families all up and down that creek," Joseph told me. "Some people called it a river because it was pretty big, bigger than it is now, because there weren't no farm ponds on it like there are now days. The land, by treaty, was Uwharrie land. Even after the war there wasn't any way that could be Kowache land, but this man Wilson, he wanted it. I'm not sure what he put in the water. I've heard strychnine, but I've also heard kerosene. People got real sick, some of them died. The families had to move off that land, some of them moving from the Reservation altogether. Tulahwassi was a good name for that creek, but we had a chief who sold it to this man Wilson when the land wasn't worth so much anymore. White people don't seem to care how bad the water is, and people just started calling it Poison Creek."

The Poison Creek Store was a white clapboard store Matt Youngblood owned, and he painted it every year or so just to make it look like a new store.

He never scraped off any old paint; he just kept painting it over and over again and it kept the store standing up. Gordon Gannon, who bought the store from him, thought that worked pretty good so he did the same thing. Hell, that store sagged from one end to the other, and a marble could roll around on the floor in there for three or four minutes. That store never did fall down; it burned down.

So me and Joe are sitting off of Highway 10, drinking a six-pack of Budweiser that he'd bought at the Poison Creek Store, and he's telling me how he's gotten drafted. We were sitting in my '54 Oldsmobile I'd bought for two hundred dollars from a white fore-man of a coal-mining operation over near Passawattan, who thought he'd driven that car into the ground. Ten o'clock in the morning and we're drinking beer and eating peanuts.

The Kowache had started another war and they wanted us to fight in it. But me and Joe didn't agree about the American Indian Movement, and we didn't agree on the Vietnam War.

"Damn," is what I said, because "I'm sorry" didn't cover it. We just sat there, looking out the windshield at nothing.

"I know what you think of this war," he said. "You're thinking it's not fair I'm the one who has to go. Well, I want to go, go kill me Vietcong. They killed Jackie, so I'll go kill a few of them for Jackie."

"Jackie signed up," I said. "He chose it."

"Yeah, he signed up, because he didn't belong. He

didn't belong on this reservation and he sure didn't belong in a white man's world. He just wanted to do something right with his life. Mom always says I was born at the wrong time, that I should have been born two hundred years ago. That's when I was supposed to be born. What else am I going to do, just sit around this fucking reservation? Hell, I could go off and make myself some money in the army. Be alright."

He wasn't alright, but Joe was going through it: cracking peanut shells between his teeth and getting ready in his mind. Joe was a warrior, and he flat out said anybody who got drafted and didn't go off to fight the Vietcong was a coward. Here he was, chowing down on peanuts, chug-a-lugging a beer, sighing and looking down at the six-pack on the seat between us, popping another beer and taking deep swigs.

"Joe," I said, "I'm going with you. I'm going to sign up. I'm going to enlist."

"What?" he said. He looked over at me like I was crazy.

"If you got to go, I'm going too. I can't let you go off by yourself," and I didn't say "and get yourself killed, like Jackie Locklear," which is what we were both thinking. "I can't let you do that. I can't let you go off to Vietnam and nobody go with you."

"Why not? What the fuck good is it going to do for both of us to go to Vietnam?" He threw a handful of peanut shells out the window.

Some white people actually think Indians *want* to get killed. Not being afraid to die and wanting to die

are two different things—and then there's dying for
no reason, which is what I thought Vietnam was. I
guess Joe would never say that. He could talk himself
into anything if he decided to.

"It could have been me that got drafted," I said,
"just the same as you."

"But it *wasn't* you," Joe said. "I got drafted and
you didn't. So I got to go off and get my ass shot at
by a bunch of Vietcong, and you don't. There's no
point in you going."

We sat there in that Oldsmobile and drank beer.
We didn't know shit about Vietnam. It was a jungle
on the other side of the world. Joe didn't know what
a communist was, except what some white farmer
drinking Pepsi Cola and eating Cheez-Its said about
communists. I had thought too that Joe would be all
for the American Indian Movement, the way he hated
white men, but he wasn't.

"Have you told Ruby yet?" I asked him.

"No," he said, took a swig and swallowed hard.

"Shit, Joe, when are you going to tell her?"

"I'll tell her."

A highway patrolman came cruising down the
road, and there we were, two Indians sitting in an old
yellow Oldsmobile pulled off by the road, holding a
six-pack down on the floorboard. We just stared
straight ahead as he went by, and I can remember Joe
saying, "Shit! Don't mess with me today."

I don't know why the cop didn't. His tail lights
came on, like he was thinking about it, but he kept on

going down the road. We sat there in that Oldsmobile and we finished off the six-pack, and after awhile Joe said he was going to go back to the house and tell Ruby how he'd gotten drafted.

Joe Bad Crow had himself a pretty good-paying job as an inspector in the oil fields. Joe wasn't a big believer in oil, but it's not like he was opposed to digging it up either. It wasn't good or bad to him, which was strange because Joe was passionate about most everything: how fucked up the Tribal Council was, what hypocrites Presbyterians were, and the Vietnam War, when it came to that. But oil didn't bother him. He had this job and he bought himself a motorcycle. It was a big old motorcycle, a 700cc Matchless bored out, so it might have been 800cc. It was one fine-looking motorcycle, but it didn't run. Joe gave Lester Keestrong a couple of cases of beer to get it running. Lester could fix anything. White people would bring their Cadillacs to him and he fixed them and made good money, and he kept all sorts of cars running on the Reservation, pieces of junk, for six-packs and fried chicken.

I helped Joe push that motorcycle over to Lester's house, a half a mile uphill, and all dirt road, until we couldn't push it anymore. I mean this was a big-ass motorcycle. We were wore out and we weren't even a quarter of the way there except Joe wasn't going to give up. This was his dream. He was going to work as an oil-field inspector for a year or two and then he was going to ride away from it all, not work for the federal government and not live on the Reservation. Somewhere inside him he hated them both, what they stood for, maybe because he saw the Reservation as the dead end of a people, and maybe the federal government because they had set the whole thing up that way. He didn't know where he was going but that was what he was going to do.

When Joe Bad Crow and me were growing up the Reservation was not a happy place. There were some ways out, like the bottle, or the needle, or suicide. Somebody could move off the Reservation and find themselves a job in a city somewhere, but there was some part of them that died when they did that. There were a couple of guys I knew, and Joe was one of them, who were going to make it off the Reservation, and still be who they were. Grady was going to do it; he was just plain smart. And Joe was going to will himself off, like when he played baseball. When he played baseball there was no pitcher who could get Joe out. If one pitch got past Joe he just doubled his will, and it got twice as hard for that pitcher to get the ball past him. If a pitcher got him out one time, the next time it would be twice as hard—until Joe got his hit.

That motorcycle was a big hope to Joe, a symbol, a big piece of metal that would take him somewhere he was wanting to go—except we couldn't get it over to Lester's house so Lester could fix it.

I sat down off the road, out of the sun, and said something like, "Joe, we can't get this motorcycle over to Lester's house. Let's just go get some help. Let's just go get that government truck you're always driving."

Joe had this good job, drove a green pick-up truck with all the gas paid, and here we were pushing that big-ass motorcycle up a hill.

"The hell you say. Get the fuck up! We can get this motorcycle over to Lester's."

I looked at him like he was crazy.

"The hell with you," I said. "You can push that fucking thing yourself."

He was ready to kill me; that was fine. That was what he was going to have to do, because I wasn't going to push that motorcycle up that dirt road anymore. But Carl Youngblood came along in his pick-up truck, headed for his brother's house because his brother had a half a pound of marijuana for him.

"What you guys doing, pushing this motorcycle up here? Damn, it's gotta be a hundred degrees out here!"

Carl had a piece of rope in his truck, a piece of rope, a tool box, and a set of golf clubs.

"What you doing with those golf clubs?" I asked.

Carl looked at Joe. He could tell Joe was losing it. He kind of smiled. Carl was a big guy and he could always make Joe laugh. "Me and Jack Nicklaus are going to play golf this weekend over at Crowsdale," he said.

I laughed, but not too hard because that could just piss Joe off. At first I thought Joe was just going to get madder, but Carl just looked at him with that big old grin of his, and Joe bust out laughing; the anger was gone. Nobody knew where it had gone but it was.

We tied the rope to the chassis of the truck and the other end to the motorcycle. Joe put it in neutral and sat on his motorcycle, and we pulled Joe and his motorcycle up the road to Lester's house. Lester had never worked on a motorcycle before, but he had worked on car engines and lawn mowers, so he figured he could do it.

Lester's girlfriend, Pam, a white woman, came out and Jackie Locklear's sister, Sherise, and later Emmons Winger came over. Carl and Joe rode back in Carl's truck and got the two cases of beer, and we drank the first case of beer while Lester cussed at that motorcycle.

"That's a fucking grounding wire, and if you guys don't get the fuck out of here I'm going to hit somebody over the head with this wrench!"

And everybody would back up a little bit and be quiet for awhile. As it turned out Lester didn't get Joe's motorcycle fixed that day.

"I can do it though," he said. "You're just going to have to get me a distributor."

"Where the fuck am I going to find a distributor for this thing? This thing is made in England, Lester!" Joe said.

"Okay," Lester said, "but you're going to at least take this gas tank and get it welded or something, because it's sure not going to hold any gas the way it is."

Joe still didn't want to use that government truck. It was an honesty thing he had. We had to hitchhike over to Landover and pay some white guy five dollars to weld the gas tank. He was a big guy. He must have weighed three hundred pounds. This guy had a short beard and blue eyes, and he asked all sorts of questions about Joe's motorcycle from just looking at that blue gas tank. He thought he might want to buy it.

"I'm not selling my motorcycle," was all Joe said.

By the time we got back to Lester's house with that gas tank the house was dark and Lester was gone. So we just left that gas tank on his front step.

It was a couple days later Joe came rumbling down the Reservation Road. He was smiling. That was the happiest I ever saw him. He gave me a ride on his motorcycle. We rode slow down the Reservation Road to the highway. When we got to the highway Joe gave it some gas, and the weight of that motorcycle moved beneath us, like a great metal horse, sure and steady. It was a sheer feeling of wild. Joe said he had no interest in his society, but when he was on that motorcycle, I think he knew the feeling. I heard him laugh, just for the joy of being on that big old motorcycle. I have learned that thoughts can weigh a person down and keep you on the ground. Flying is a feeling; there's no thinking to it. It's the greatest freedom. This is part of what the owl knows, what the owl has taught me.

Good luck and bad luck can sometimes be the same thing, or bad luck can be good luck. One way or the other, Joe Bad Crow ran into a hell of a streak of something, and as hard as it was on him, it was that much and harder on Ruby. They were pretty much separated, but, at the same time, trying to find out if that was the right thing to do, and that motorcycle kind of saved Joe's life. And strange as it may be, sometimes life ain't what it seems.

It was my sister Ruby who got me interested in the American Indian Movement. She was something of a paradox the way she didn't like to hear anybody say anything bad about Chief Billy Farmer, and yet she got involved in AIM. She got into it in a big way, maybe because it was what she needed in tough times. I'm not sure Joe Bad Crow was really staying at the house at that time; he was never over there when I went over there. I didn't know then where he was staying but I was beginning to know it wasn't at the house with Ruby and Anthony John.

In the seventies there was a lot of talk on the Reservation about Indian sovereignty. It was an idea, and I don't know where it came from but it caught on. One Saturday night there was going to be a gathering at the Infirmary about Indian sovereignty, and maybe Russell Means was going to be there, only it didn't happen at the Infirmary because Chief Billy didn't want it to. The gathering ended up at the church, and Russell Means never did show up. That was the night Sun Susie disappeared.

I went down there with Gettis Strange, my sister Ruby, and this white guy named Bucky that Gettis knew. I don't what I was expecting but Joe Bad Crow wasn't there that night, and at the time I didn't think anything of it because I knew the way he felt about that kind of thing—AIM, Vietnam, whatever. It was that day, that afternoon, some white guy pulled out on Joe out on Highway 10. Joe was probably never going to walk again, never get off the Reservation, much less go off to the other side of the world and fight the Vietcong. Army doctor was going to say he was 4-F, because he was going to have a steel pin in his leg. We were all getting caught up in something bigger than us, but that night, none of us knew about any of that, not Joe, not Sun Susie.

Bucky was a photographer from Florida and was kind of famous because he took a picture of an AIM member waving a flag while he was standing on an oil truck somewhere off in Utah or Wyoming. It got picked up by *Look* magazine; I've got it pinned to corkboard on my bathroom wall. The man's identified as being from AIM, but you can't see his face because his back is turned to you. He's standing on top of a gasoline tanker and waving the red flag, the flag of all Indian people. It's a black-and-white picture but it was a red flag, and behind him is a silver-blue valley, the high peak of a distant mountain rimmed with light. It's a sacred mountain. You can see that in the photograph, the sun shining across a valley, appearing like water in a silver lake. It's an amazing picture! You can feel the wind blowing across the top of that oil tanker, filling the folds of that red flag. The spirit is blowing like a gale on a mountain, a wailing wind, the voices of people. It's a song of sorrow.

And here's Bucky, this tall blond guy with the thigh-bone of a chicken he's twirling between his lips, wearing a red bandana around his blond head and a kind of happy-go-lucky white-boy grin. He's a real asshole.

There were a lot of people there; the churchyard was crawling with people and cars parked all which-a-way. We ended up about fifty yards down the church road. There were even people from out of state there, and I remember Gettis kept saying, "Damn! This is alright!"

There were a bunch of young white people there too, hippies and whatnot, back-to-the-landers, counterculture this and counterculture that, young people looking for something. They were drawn to the reservations. There was still hope on the reservations. That might seem like a strange thing, because sometimes it seemed like the Reservation was the last place there was any hope. There's Indian guys too, not Uwharrie, walking around waving the American flag and wearing U.S. Army shirts and shooting their mouths off about how great America is, but there was a whole other way of thinking, that Vietnam was just one more scam and just one more way to use the Indian, or whoever it was convenient to use. All the windows of the church were open, because it was hot, with people leaning over the windowsills to see and hear what's going on. There were more people outside the church than in, and there was some hooting and hollering. They got a PA system set up. We got us some barbecue and some ice tea, and me and Gettis, we just sat down on the slab covering the well house while Ruby and this guy Bucky go off around the back of the church to find out what's going on. While we were sitting there on the top of the well house we started hearing how maybe Russell Means wasn't going to come at all.

There were six or seven people outside sitting at a big drum, and all the sticks were coming up and hitting the drum at the same time, everybody singing songs they'd never sung before. They didn't know where the songs came from, or how they all knew them, but the songs were there. There was dancing in the churchyard. After awhile Ruby and Bucky came back and said how it was going to be somebody else, not Russell Means, who was going to speak, and that they were going to move the microphones to the church steps so everybody could hear.

Gettis was sour on Russell Means. He'd heard how Russell Means was coming that night and had been hoping to find out for himself if Russell Means was as big an asshole as Gettis thought he was.

"Fuck, he ain't no leader of an American Indian Movement," Gettis said. "He ain't no founder either. People doing all the work and he's just coming around here getting credit for it. He's a fucking personality, a real Bob Barker."

Gettis was a genuine split personality. Sometimes nothing could phase him, like he'd just come out of a sweat lodge or he'd gotten himself laid. Other times though, and you never knew when it was going to be, he'd get all worked up, get on to Nixon or Eisenhower or something. "What a son of a bitch Eisenhower was!" Gettis would say, and he couldn't have been more than eight or nine years old when

Eisenhower was president, but he knew all about Eisenhower. "Signs a bill to put an end to all the reservations. What is that? The termination laws the U.S. government passed took away millions of acres of lands belonging to Indian peoples. With a stroke of the pen the U.S. got more land than changes hands in most wars between whole nations. If the Arab states of the Mid-East could do the same thing, they could eliminate Israel altogether by saying they wanted to buy it, or just declaring it an Arab state, or evicting Israelis. They could just say, 'Sure! You can stay. But you got to be Arab, be part of the Arab nation.' It's the same with us. 'Oh yeah, we're U.S. citizens! Oh boy, let's wave that American flag.' I can hear Eisenhower now, 'I have a *vision* for this country.' Shit, that ain't no vision; that's nothing more than a bunch of white guys in a back room drawing up plans for high rises with a view of the shopping center, move us into the cities so we can learn how to be white people, play golf, that kind of shit. Interstates was his idea too, four lanes to everywhere to keep the communists from overrunning the country."

This guy Bucky, the photographer, is trying to take pictures of all this, but some guy wearing an army shirt and a red bandana doesn't want him to because he's white and tells him to move off. I was thinking there was going to be a fight; tempers were running high. Bucky somehow caught Ruby's attention, and his thing is universities, and he finds out about Ruby and Brigham Young, and he gets going on how universities are "like the farm leagues for the establishment." She's eating it up, maybe because she dropped out of school, I don't know, but there's so much bullshit going on I don't know what to think, and Ruby's into this tall-ass white guy from Florida, and it isn't long before he goes on from colleges to talking about picking oranges and the welfare state.

So now it's Gettis Strange and this white guy Bucky going on and on, and the drum was pounding and the blood was rising. Somewhere off to the west there was thunder and the wind stirred in the trees. A young woman said, "Man, it's going to rain like hell."

And somebody said, "Don't say that! Don't even think it."

I turned around. It's Thomas Matoas Paint. Thomas has a feather, a hawk feather, and he's holding it up to the sky, motioning gently with his hand. "No, not tonight! We need you, but not tonight. Come back tomorrow."

The tops of the trees were swaying and the drum was pounding and it was getting darker than dark. By then there were flashes of lightning in the sky and the thunder was rolling. That storm was about to hit. You know the feeling: when you know you have about ten seconds to find cover and then the bottom is going to drop out. Only thing is, that storm just went away, just like Thomas asked it to. It rained everywhere else that night, a hard rain, the kind of rain that washes out roads and blows down trees, but not at the New Presbyterian Church. That night the storm went around us. Thomas Matoas Paint did that with a hawk feather.

Thomas was always saying how white people think the only spirits embodied in the world are their own; our people have become apt to believe them. But like Thomas said, everything has spirit: the mountains have spirit, every plant, every animal, the insects and the birds, they all have spirit—and a storm has spirit.

"Storms have a will, but you don't command storms to go around; you ask them to go around," Thomas Matoas Paint said that night. He reasoned with them: "We really need this meeting tonight. It would be a whole lot better if you would go around us and rain somewhere else tonight where they're not having a big meeting."

Maybe it rained on Chief Billy's house.

Some people had already started running for their cars, and some people tried to push into the church because the winds had started blowing the leaves and dust around. It never did rain. People who'd gone to sit in their cars came back, and after the storm had passed Gary Yellow Knife, carrying his favorite gourd rattle with a turkey feather tied to the handle, spoke a blessing, Ruth Upchurch standing by his side, holding his elbow, making sure he didn't fall over. Gary had a balance problem he didn't tell anybody or himself about. He was dressed in full regalia, got on his bonnet and his bone shirt, his leggings and his moccasins decorated with porcupine quills Ruth had made for him, and he looked halfway between not knowing where he was and like he had just come from dreaming the universe. Gary Yellow Knife never seemed like he was looking at you out of both eyes. One eye was always looking somewhere else.

Gary Yellow Knife surprised everybody. He's a traditional and he was talking about the BIA and everything else, how the government built shit we didn't need, and uranium mines we didn't need. We didn't have uranium mines and I don't know if Gary Yellow Knife was confused about where or when he was, or if there was something political I didn't know about.

Then the representative from AIM spoke. It wasn't Russell Means; it was this guy named Small Dog, and he was one skinny Indian. Skinny arms, skinny legs, skinny and sharp-faced like the stare of a snake. You couldn't tell how old he was. Maybe he'd done some hard living; he might've been about thirty or he might've been fifty. I don't know. He was Comanche or Kiowa. He was wearing snakeskin boots and blue jeans and a purple polyester button shirt, but it wasn't buttoned, and you could see tattoos, except they looked more like burns in a pattern—Comanche or something—on his chest and his arms. He never quite straightened up, moved around on the cement steps like a boxer, bending his knees and weaving around, looking at people, talking to people. Snake energy.

"We have to wake up! The government, the oil companies, the silent majority, the good-old-boys club, Hollywood, the BIA, big business, whoever, they are all counting on us to stay asleep. They'd roll over us with steamrollers while our bones slept in the dirt. We got to wake up!"

He told us about how the governors of two states signed over Indian land to the energy corporations, how Union Carbide obtained exploratory drilling and mining rights and not one Indian tribe had been consulted or received a single penny. The energy crisis was profitable and the U.S. government was again turning its one big eye to the Indian people and our land. Small Dog held up a one-dollar bill and showed everybody the one big eye on top of the pyramid.

He kept talking about being awake, asked us if we thought anybody in Philadelphia, Atlanta, Los Angeles, Detroit or Dallas cared about a bunch of Indians on a reservation in the middle of nowhere. If we didn't care about ourselves, why should they?

Snake energy is tricky business. Some people, like Chief Billy, never can stop thinking about self-promotion, and with that white asshole of a photographer hitting on my sister and taking pictures and getting right up underneath Small Dog while he was talking, I wondered if this wasn't all some kind of publicity stunt.

But Small Dog didn't try to talk us into getting ourselves arrested or shot. Instead, he said it wasn't going to be short and it wasn't going to be easy, that it was going to be a long hard road, but that it was the Red Road. He said he was there to tell us the facts; tomorrow or the next day, he'd be gone. That impressed me, because some people want to be leaders too much.

That night at the church Small Dog told us about

how a tribe possesses a nation-within-a-nation status: sovereignty. A government, from the U.S. government to the Tribal Council, can tell you what a treaty means, but they will never tell you that treaties formalize a nation-to-nation relationship between the federal government and a tribe. U.S. laws do not apply in Indian country, and there can be no such thing as eminent domain. What he said was exciting; it was new. I had never really stopped to think about it, how when the U.S. government said they wanted to look for uranium on our reservation, they said it was a matter of "national security." But *our* nation was safe and we could decide for ourselves how to make those decisions. A tribe can have a Tribal Council or not.

Small Dog reminded us of how many times we had been at a Tribal Council meeting where there were more white people than Indians: "That's not a Tribal Council meeting, that's a hearing." He asked us if we had any idea how our Tribal Council had been established, or had it been something forced on us by the U.S. Congress and the Indian Reorganization Act of 1941. The U.S. government wanted to get around the way Indians made decisions, and so they made tribes change the way we did things.

There were some of Chief Billy Farmer's thugs there, and I guess they weren't too happy about what Small Dog was saying, and about the time Small Dog started talking about mineral rights Chief Billy's goons muscled their way to the microphone. They started telling everybody it was time to go home, saying the Tribal Council hadn't approved a non-native speaking on reservation land.

"What do you mean non-native? He's Chippewa," Lees Kramer said. Lees was a big man, with a big old horse face and a big old body from drinking a lot of Budweiser.

"Chippewa, Cherokee—it doesn't matter. He's not Uwharrie; that means he's a non-native."

It was some Chief Billy bullshit, and then the power went out. Microphone, lights inside the church, everything. People started going home. That's what Chief Billy's goons wanted and that's what happened, and by the time things got sorted out most everybody had left.

The next day Sun Susie comes up missing. Nobody knew it right away, but after a couple of days Aunt Ida started asking around, because Sun Susie hadn't come by, and Aunt Ida had had to feed the horses. Sun Susie had just up and disappeared, and I hadn't thought about it but she hadn't been at the AIM gathering, though that wasn't surprising.

Sun Susie wasn't at her house or anywhere else Aunt Ida looked, and some people started talking about keeping an eye out for crows and where they were gathering. We'd heard about that kind of stuff with people associated with AIM, and the way Carl Youngblood found June Goins because his truck broke down and he noticed crows down in the bottom of a ravine. Nothing like that had happened. I think she was buried somewhere up behind Old Man's Back and nobody was going to know anything about anything up there.

Joe Bad Crow didn't get off the Reservation getting drafted into the Army, didn't get off the Reservation on his motorcycle. That day of the AIM gathering at the church he had the motorcycle accident, some white guy pulls out on him on Highway 10. By the time I heard about it Joe Bad Crow'd been on the operating table for four hours and was released into intensive care. He was in the hospital over in Landover. Lester and Sherise gave me a ride and we went up there but Joe didn't say anything. His head was bandaged and his face was black and blue. He had broken his leg real bad. All he could do was open his eyes. He could see us but he couldn't say anything. He moaned. His eyelids fluttered and then they closed. We thought he was going to die, but he didn't.

The next day they said Joe was going to make it but he would probably never walk again. I couldn't believe it. I remember wondering if maybe it would be better if he would just die. I couldn't see Joe living without being able to walk, to run. I didn't know then how a person can be a warrior in their mind, how that's the only place a person really is a warrior.

The cops said if Joe hadn't been so athletic, he would have died. They said anybody else would have. The way they figured it Joe's motorcycle hit right over the back wheel, and Joe didn't have much time, but he jumped straight up off that motorcycle and cleared the roof of the van—all except his right leg which hit it hard going by, which is what they thought broke it so bad—and then Joe had flown down the road some 160 feet. That's when he'd gotten all the bruises.

It was a week before Joe spoke, at least before he spoke to me. It was hard. I knew his dream. I knew it better than anyone. In those days, we had the same dream. It was a dream without words, a feeling. We had felt it on the back of that motorcycle; it was a confirmation for us that the dream was real: spirit moving in the wildness as it was before, something a white man would never teach us. There was nothing to be free of until the white man came.

Me and Ruby went up to see Joe one day and he was talking. By then it was like she could only love him from a distance, and being in the same room with Joe was a pain she couldn't bear. She didn't tell me; it was just what I could feel and see, smoke off a dying fire, and I knew her heart was breaking in two.

I couldn't believe the first words Joe said to me.

"How's the motorcycle?"

I shook my head. "Not good."

He took in air through his nose, like a sigh, and he breathed out through his nose, like a sigh.

"Warren," he said, "when I get out of this hospital I'm going to kill that white bastard."

"Joe," I said, "they're saying you're not going to walk again."

"Fuck what they say!" he said. He sat up. He tried to move his leg. He tried to move it in his mind but all he got was pain and he lay back down. He was grimacing, and breathing hard through his nose. Most of the bruises on his face didn't look so bad by then. He looked like himself, only he couldn't move his leg. He lay there and I could see his jaw set. He said it again.

"When I get out of this hospital I'm going to kill that white bastard! I'm going right from this hospital bed to a jail bed."

Neither me or Ruby said anything. I knew what he meant, and Ruby just sort of resigned herself that this was the whole problem between them.

"Do you know what that fucker did?" he said.

I just shook my head. I knew he was talking about the white guy driving the car. It was a week later, but I knew who he was talking about.

"Do you know what that fucker did?" he said again, hard and excited. The muscles of his arms were standing out like cords. His face was rigid with rage, but it hurt. It hurt to be angry. He was in that kind of pain. He spoke slowly, from his determination.

"I'm riding down the road. There's a dirt side road, a stop sign and a white Chevrolet van sitting there. He's just there, like he's waiting for me. This white guy and his girlfriend sitting in his van, watching me coming down the road. The fucker is watching me! I'm going forty-five, maybe fifty-five miles an hour, I don't know. It's all in slow motion now. Maybe I think he likes my motorcycle. Maybe that's why I didn't see it. This asshole sees me coming down the road. I know he sees me. I don't know, maybe I'm a hundred feet from him by then. He's got this smile on his face, and I don't know what it means. I do now. Warren, this guy was looking right at me. I see him put that van in gear. I don't know what he's doing. He's smiling. I'm riding by and this fucker just fucking plain pulls out! He's smiling at me. This mind-fucker looks at me and he pulls out. It's my fucking life and he pulls out!"

Joe stopped. I think he had to, because reality was coming down on him pretty hard. The doctors were telling him he's never going to walk again, and the cops were telling him he was going too fast and they're going to give Joe a ticket, and he's going to have go to court when he gets out of the hospital. Joe had a driver's license but he didn't have a license plate on his motorcycle because he hadn't gotten it in the mail yet, and the cops weren't going to be trying to find this guy. The police did come and talk to Joe, and got a full description of the man, but nothing ever came of it. This Indian had been speeding; he'd gotten what he deserved.

"I tell you I'm not going to any fucking court because I'm going to fucking jail. I'm killing the fucking son of a bitch."

We didn't say anything because I guess me and Ruby figured if we did Joe would just get more dead set on killing the asshole. I can hear what he would say. "I'll give him a fair fight. Just me and him. No guns, no knifes. Just one Indian against one white guy. Motherfucker!"

Even then we didn't tell Joe the guy who pulled

out on him didn't even call in the accident. That was some salesman from Texas who came along and found Joe twisting in pain in the middle of the road. We just listened.

"You know what, Warren?" Joe kept on. "The fucking cops came in here the day after the accident, Saturday, asking their fucking questions. You know what those motherfuckers say? They say the guy didn't see me and that I was going too fast. Now how do those motherfuckers know I'm going too fast and that the fucking asshole can't see me? Did he tell them that? Where is that motherfucker anyway? That's fucking white cops for you. Well, I sure did see him; I know what the motherfucker looks like, and I'm going to find that motherfucking asshole and kill the fucker."

But then Joe just changed right there, started laughing to himself, fantasizing on what could balance his universe. He said, "I think I'll cut his balls off first." It wasn't quite a laugh really. He had to keep his mouth closed because it hurt him too much to laugh.

I watched him. I could read his mind turning. They still had him on morphine or something, and it was like he was underwater. His mind was trying to figure it all out but he couldn't. He pulled his hands across his face, like he was going to try to tear off his own skin, pulling at his hair like he was trying to rip it out, and his eyes went wild. He tried to get up, pull the tubes out of his arms, but it hurt too much, and there was all that not knowing where to go or how to find a man who already had two weeks lead and no one looking for him.

Ruby was pretty shaken up. She still loved Joe, but life is more than that, and that whole time Joe had been talking he had hardly looked at her, like Joe didn't want her there, and so the way he dealt with it was to pretend she wasn't. It was like they were strangers to each other. It wasn't silence between them, it was emptiness with no words for it.

Joe was going to get his big tryout in baseball that summer. It didn't happen. He'd been playing semi-pro, hitchhiking to games or borrowing Sun Susie's car. Ruby had figured that out long before I did. To drive Sun Susie's car was why Joe had gotten a license. The whole time he'd been with Ruby he never had a license, she just drove him everywhere, or he got a ride with somebody else, or he walked. It's not something I know about but there is some kind of basic difference between a girlfriend and a wife, at least for Joe there was. Joe didn't ever have to go to court because it turned out the license plate was in the mail. Turned out too the white doctors were wrong about Joe. They said he'd never walk again. Joe not only walked again, he ran.

When Joe came back from the hospital in the back of Carl Youngblood's truck, struggling and nearly falling when he slid off the tailgate and onto his crutches, I knew he was going to walk again. I didn't know he was going to run again but I knew he was going to walk. Joe wouldn't let anybody help him get out of the back of Carl's truck.

Anthony John was standing by the gate; I don't know, maybe he was nine or ten years old at the time. His face was twisted in pain while he watched his father walk towards him. Joe was on those crutches, grunting, but he stopped when he got to Anthony John, and propped himself up and raised one crutch into the air, showing him how it was going to be. He smiled at Anthony John, and Anthony John smiled back. When I saw Joe going into the house Anthony John was still standing by the gate. He was crying.

I can't say how hard all that was on Ruby. She knew Joe needed somebody to take care of him, and I don't know how they worked it out, or if they even ever talked to each other the whole time he was laid up on crutches. In those days Joe hardly spoke anyway, and I didn't know if it was because of Ruby or his own leg, or the fact that some white man had probably murdered his girlfriend and tried to kill him with no real reason why. Or what might have been if none of it had happened. No explanation, it was just his life. I'd go over there to their house and he'd be walking across the room using one crutch. He'd be walking up to the mailbox on one crutch. Walking down the road on one crutch.

One day we were going to walk up the road; I don't even remember why. Maybe we were just going to walk up to the end of the road. We did that sometimes. No reason, just the end of the road, where our road joined Reservation Road. There was a sign nailed onto a tree pointing up the Reservation Road, saying Scofields, because they lived up there. So did a lot of other people but Joe Scofield wanted to keep his seat on the Council so he had a sign up on an oak tree. Anyway, Joe and I were going to walk up to the end of the road one evening after supper, and he said, "Let's race."

It was pretty near dark.

I looked at Joe like he was crazy. He saw that and it just made him more determined to race, so he said, "C'mon, I mean it. Let's go. Let's race! Say go!"

And he crouched down in a painful awful-looking way, favoring the leg, and he wasn't even running yet.

"Joe, you got a steel pin in your leg! You're not supposed to be running. Doctors don't want you to be running no race."

"Fuck the doctors!" Joe said. "If I listen to them I'm just gonna sit on my ass the rest of my life. I'm not going to do that. Hell with that! Now c'mon, let's go. Say go!"

I sighed. I didn't want to run a race against Joe, not with a steel pin in his leg, but I didn't see any way around it, so I said, "Okay. Go!"

We were running in the twilight. I didn't have to run too hard to beat Joe that night, but he did *run*. It wasn't pretty, but he was *running*. It wasn't that fast, but it sure was faster than I thought it could be. I wasn't running hard but he wasn't that far behind me.

The thing was, when he got to where I was standing in the road near that tree with the Scofield sign on it, Joe was still running as hard as he could. He'd already lost the race, but he was running the same as if he was only a half-step behind me. It hurt just to look at him running, looked like his leg was about to break again or something, and he was breathing hard from his nose and wincing from pain. He bent over double there in the gathering darkness. He was dog-tired, but when he lifted up his head, he was smiling.

A couple of nights later Joe and I raced again, and he got closer.

The funny thing about it all was, Joe thought he was supposed to die. He was supposed to go off to Vietnam and get himself killed like Jackie Locklear. Only thing was it didn't happen. A lot of guys were getting drafted; most of them didn't want to go. I didn't want to go. But Joe gets the idea, after all he'd been through, that he's still going to go to Vietnam. Here it is, he's been on crutches for two months, and the doctor says he's never going to run again, and he tries to report. He said he wanted to kill somebody and he didn't want it to be a white man because they sure would put him in jail, so it might as well be some Vietcong he killed. That was legal.

He went and had a physical and the white doctor said, "You ain't going to Vietnam; you got a steel pin in your leg. You're 4-F."

Some people I know would've been celebrating, but not Joe. He looked like his mother had died. Here was his chance to finally kill somebody and get himself killed, and they wouldn't let him do it. He was all the time saying it would be better for everybody if he just went away. For awhile Joe went crazy. A lot of people think it's wrong to go crazy, but sometimes a person just has to do it. They're still inside the circle and they have to go crazy. If they didn't go crazy their souls wouldn't be released, their souls wouldn't fly where they're meant to go. I knew Joe doing what he did had something to do with balancing the universe. It had all the marks of that.

One day Joe took Thomas Matoas Paint's old Rambler station wagon, borrowed it without telling Thomas. That wasn't so unusual, but the next thing we knew, Joe was in jail. He'd been driving down the Brownsville Highway, Highway 101, clipping off mailboxes with that old Rambler station wagon. I don't know how fast he was going but he snapped off a half-mile of mailboxes and tore the shit out of the bottom of Thomas's car. People were saying he was going to jail for twenty years for destroying govern-ment property. That worried me some because I knew Joe did what he said and he always said he'd rather be dead than in jail.

It never went to court though. It's a good thing because if they'd asked him if he'd been clipping off mailboxes with Thomas's old Rambler, Joe'd've told them he had. He was that pissed off. Grady Locklear was his lawyer, came all the way from St. Louis and stayed at his mom's house. Grady did all the talking; Joe didn't say a word.

A night or two later Joe came over and we raced to the Scofield sign. Joe beat me in that footrace.

Every thief has a family. Half the Tribal Council was Chief Billy Farmer's family. You could tell when they were over there watching TV or eating fried chicken together because it looked like a parking lot; they had more cars than anybody. Chief Billy lived in a ranch house with a ramp running up to the front door before anybody ever thought of handicap access. This was because of Chief Billy's wife, Alma Farmer. She wasn't alcoholic, she was bulimic, and at one time had been as big as a barn. She still went to AA meetings at the Infirmary. They built that house in the fifties when the tribe signed its first lease with the Uncle Sam Petroleum Company for oil exploration on the New Reservation.

At one time we had a summer chief and a winter chief. The summer chief was in charge of what went on in the summertime, and the winter chief would be his advisor. In winter it was the other way around. Aunt Ida, Mercy Cleary, Grandfather and Grandmother all knew about that, but since the coming of the church—or the coming of the oil—the government is vested in an elected chief and a council. And, at one time, practically all the affairs of importance—war, medicine, hunting, agriculture— were controlled by the secret societies: the Society of the Grouse, the Crow, the Lizard, the Trout, the Mountain Lion, the Owl. But all that has been ending for some time now. Now we have drought; the crops fail, and the Tribal Council says they don't know anything about that.

Chief Billy had an office in the Legion Hall; he wasn't hardly ever there. That was kind of a good thing, and if you wanted to know what was going on, what had happened in the last few days if you didn't know, you'd go to the Legion Hall. This was a one-story cinder-block building built in the twenties with the idea of bringing American life to the Reservation, with display cases for trophies and stuff because the American Legion sponsored a youth baseball league. The Reservation team won a bunch of trophies, especially when Joe Bad Crow was playing, but most of the first-place trophies got stolen, the glass broken by some drunk white guys pissed off because they hadn't won a Little League baseball game or something. In the seventies the glass got put back in, and some replica trophies got made but nobody ever knew what happened to those other trophies.

The American Legion sponsored all sorts of stuff: football, basketball, Little League baseball, Pony League, softball, whatever. A bunch of us had ourselves a softball team called the Ghost Dogs. I guess we thought that might put some kind of whammy on other teams. We played in a league with mostly white teams, and then there was us and a team from the prison. They were all black guys. We were good. We had Joe Bad Crow, he played left field before his motorcycle accident, and a real good shortstop, Joe Cross, and Gene Middle Dawn, and the Phoenix brothers. I played center field, and Thomas Matoas Paint hardly played at all because he was so big, old and fat. But when he played Thomas was the catcher. He looked like a catcher, with a big belly and everything, but he couldn't hit a lick. He just loved to talk so he enjoyed the game, whether he was playing or not, and it didn't matter who we were playing. When we were playing the hippies he talked to them about visions, and the energy coming up through the ground right by third base or something, but then when we played the mill workers, he talked to them about life, just life in general, whatever. He even found something to talk about with the Chevy dealership team. They were a bunch of assholes, but Thomas would talk to them. They wouldn't talk back much, because they were all white and uptight, but he'd just go on about the weather, or some neat pick-up truck he'd seen, and pretty soon he'd work him-self up to unusual occurrences, UFOs or strange things about the weather a car salesman could never explain.

I remember before one game, and we might have been playing that Chevy dealership team, Gene Middle Dawn got this idea we should paint ourselves up. We usually got to the game thirty or forty-five minutes early so we could warm up, but this game we all painted our faces. Everybody was painting each other's faces with little paintbrushes and Gene looked around and saw Thomas Matoas Paint was just sitting at the end of the bleachers watching everybody.

"Thomas," Gene said, "you got to paint up your face."

"No," Thomas said. "I'm gathering up internal energy. Painting my face is an external act. It would give energy away. It would take away from the energy inside and put it on the outside."

"What for? Why are you gathering up internal energy?" Gene asked.

"I'm not a medicine man," Thomas Matoas Paint said, "but I am a medicine man in training. It's not time for me to paint my face up. When it's time, you'll know it."

Gene Middle Dawn just stood there for a moment taking that in, then he said, with a smile, "I can respect that."

So Thomas didn't paint his face for the game like everybody else. Those white guys thought we were one bunch of crazy Indians, but when Thomas got up to bat everybody saw he didn't have his face painted up like everybody else, and somebody from the Chevy dealership yelled from their bench, "Hey Injun! How come you don't have your face painted like everybody else?" They thought we were all crazy, but I guess they kind of liked it too.

"I'm their father," Thomas called back.

Everybody laughed at that.

But the next game, when nobody had their face painted, Thomas Matoas Paint showed up with his face painted blue and green, with lightning bolts on his cheeks.

"Thomas, what're you doing?" Rudy Goins asked him.

"I didn't want you guys to think I didn't love you," Thomas said.

The Tribal Council met in the Legion Hall. There was a big meeting room and a recreation room with a pool table. The pool table was a story in itself. I don't know where it came from, but there were little stories all over that pool table: beer stains on the felt; notches in the wood; samples of marble a salesman left stuck under one leg because Joe Bad Crow slammed that leg with a cue stick one night when he missed a shot that cost him five bucks. There was a tear in the felt—if it was felt—a good foot and a half long where it was said a hook on a bungie cord snagged in a cigarette burn when somebody was trying to glue a loose bumper back on.

You weren't supposed to have beer in the Legion Hall, but we'd take it in there in brown bags. Chief Billy wasn't too keen on beer in the Legion Hall, but I never knew of him being in the poolroom. He'd never show his face in there. The poolroom was where a lot of stuff got talked about, though we never had like an official AIM meeting—we were never that organized—but that's where we talked about it. The morning after that meeting at the church, that night Sun Susie disappeared, there was some of us in that poolroom talking with Small Dog. The inside door had a small piece of cracked rectangular glass—somebody had chucked a pool ball at it once—and I remember looking up from where I was sitting against the wall and seeing Chief Billy's face through the cracked glass. He was looking in, just watching. He never liked young people on the Reservation gravitating to AIM or anything that had anything to do with questioning who was controlling land or resources. Chief Billy was mostly watching Small Dog, who was standing with the outside door open, and rolling cigarettes and smoking a Camel, and blowing perfect smoke rings. Small Dog was one skinny Indian. He had skinny arms and you couldn't tell how old he was. Maybe he'd done some hard living; I don't know. Some people can stare straight into the sun. Small Dog had a hardness to him, a good person to have as a friend, and had a lot of snake energy, so that when he looked over at the door and saw Chief Billy looking in, Chief Billy left and didn't come back.

We never got organized, not the way Small Dog was talking about, but I remember where I was July 26th—that was 1975. It was a hot, sticky night. Ruby and me were at Carl Youngblood's while he was working on somebody's old Ford truck; I was holding the flashlight. Gettis Strange and Carl's brother Cleve were there too. By this time Gettis had changed his mind about Russell Means and was even talking about going off to Oregon and getting involved in some AIM activity out there. That old Ford truck had a good radio and Wanda Upchurch was sitting up in the driver's seat trying to find a good country station when she came across the news on a station out of Rapid City, South Dakota. We never got a station out of Rapid City, South Dakota. Radio didn't come in good up in those mountains, because of minerals, but the signal came in that day. The clouds or the earth's magnetic field were coordinating themselves. The night before Wanda Upchurch said she'd seen the Northern Lights driving back from the Presbyterian Hospital. The radio signal was there for us.

We all felt it; it was like we all had relatives there at Pine Ridge. I didn't know much about the Pine Ridge Reservation; South Dakota was like on the other side of the world. But we knew about Wounded Knee a couple of years before and how Nixon had promised the Lakota that he'd work with them, if they lay down their arms, and then he turned around and said that days of treaties were over. A couple of years later and here was a standoff again between Indians and FBI. Tribal cops were involved. It had been going on for weeks and then all hell broke loose. There were a bunch of stories coming out of Pine Ridge, but that night on the radio, we could hear it—the news coming out of Rapid City.

The signal never did come in great, and Wanda kept messing with the signal while we were trying to listen.

"Leave it alone, Wanda!" Carl shouted a couple of times, but she kept messing with it.

Gettis, or Cleve, was for driving off to find a TV but everybody agreed there wouldn't be much on TV about a shoot-out on an Indian Reservation in South Dakota unless it was going to say what a wonderful bunch of guys the FBI was. Carl had tuna fish and Wanda went inside and fixed us up some tuna fish sandwiches with mayonnaise. We sat outside drinking beer and talking, listening to the radio. The signal got better. They started mixing country western music in with reports from South Dakota, what Lakota sources were saying, and what the FBI was saying. I kept looking north for the Northern Lights but I never saw them.

Best we could tell from the radio was that a couple hundred FBI agents, goons and BIA police are trying to kill any Indian who didn't walk out with his hands up. There were women and children involved. They'd all been living in tents for weeks and then a couple of FBI agents decide they are going to arrest somebody named Jimmy Eagle for taking cowboy boots off of a drunk white guy in a bar a couple of nights before. I mean there was a Mexican standoff going on with rifles all around and these two dumb asses decide they're going to waltz in and arrest an Indian for stealing cowboy boots.

We lost the signal, and the next day we got the news sixty-some Indians were murdered, all of them affiliated with AIM. There's a manhunt going on because the FBI has decided one man was responsible: Leonard Peltier. He defended women and children from fifty or sixty FBI agents who wanted to turn Pine Ridge into the gunfight at the OK Corral and he's the one they're going to nail like Jesus because he's the one who won't come out with his hands up. Nobody knew where he was, until he gave himself up.

That's American justice; two FBI agents get themselves killed in a shoot-out because they want to get a good-old-boy's cowboy boots back, and Leonard Peltier's in prison today serving two life terms, like Jesus, carrying the sins of everybody.

Young people were breathing life back into the Reservation, and Chief Billy and his Tribal Council just kept saying we were being stupid, and Leonard Peltier got what he deserved. That's the way Chief Billy was; he played it careful every step of the way.

Chief Billy drove a silver pick-up truck most of the time, but he had a white Buick Le Sabre too, one of those with the big fins. He got that Buick when the tribe sold timber rights on the Urapati-ton, the Range of Light. There's some beautiful country up there. We got new nets for the rims on the outdoor basketball court, got the lines repainted, and Chief Billy got a new Buick. He didn't drive it much, and made a point of saying how he bought that car out of his own personal money and the reason he bought it was to impress white businessmen. He said he was showing them that the Uwharrie didn't need their money, because in some back-asswards way Chief Billy thought white businessmen would offer more money for the timber they wanted if they thought we didn't need the money.

He drove that Buick down to the end of his driveway to pick up his mail and he'd park down there like he was reading it, sit there for half an hour or more smoking cigarettes because Alma didn't like him smoking at all. But Chief Billy wasn't reading his mail because he had his eyeglasses on. He wore glasses that he bought at the drug store, not because he needed them, but because he thought it made him look more official when he was talking with white people. That was his big joke with us when it came around to another election, how good he was at getting stuff we wanted from the white people. He'd been chief since before I was born.

He couldn't see shit through those eyeglasses though, and if you walked in front of his Buick on the way to the mailbox, Chief Billy'd make a point of waving at you first thing, smiling that big-ass smile of his, sitting there in his white '58 Buick.

Chief Billy was one of those who liked to make a point of being friendly, like you could trust him, but when he was being friendly was just the time you shouldn't trust him. He was good at talking with white people and trying to get money for the tribe; white people couldn't read him. And he didn't look so much like an Indian, not like a mean-ass Indian anyway, like those pictures of Geronimo. No, Chief Billy looked like a friendly Indian, wore his light-brown hair loose and long under a cowboy hat, like a white woman. He had thin lips like a white woman and he smiled a lot, like he didn't have the faintest notion that anything was going on with tribal funds and lands and oil rights. He knew he was smiling, like he was using muscles to make himself smile. That kind of thing is scary when you think about it.

The thing was, every time Chief Billy Farmer needed a new car for his brother, or a trailer for one of his relatives, or an addition to his house, he'd sell off timber on tribal lands, and we'd get some new nets, or a couple of new road signs, or a guard rail. Oh, we'd know about tribal meetings and all, but somehow, every time there was going to be a meeting about anything big, like boundaries, timber rights or a connector road for the white people, we never heard about it. Not until afterwards and then he'd say, "Where have you been? We had a meeting about that last month. I told you about that."

And he'd walk away and that'd be it. Next time he saw you he'd make like nothing ever happened except you went away with that uneasy feeling that there was a whole lot more he hadn't told you than he had.

He was always saying how he wanted to hear what everybody wanted, what was good for the tribe, but he had the same grin for everything. He had this way of lifting his head up off his shoulders and grinning at you, like he was saying, "You can't tell if I'm lying or not," or "When you get outta sight I'm going to do whatever I want to because I'm the chief. You're not." Chief Billy's big thing was being savvy to how the white community worked, and he had a lot of people convinced that without him looking out for tribal interests, we were going to get the very short end of a very long stick.

He kept saying that oil being found on the New Reservation was going to change everything. He got people into believing in a future—like white people—and not really being happy with what was right here. The Kowache celebrate something that happened two thousand years ago, and for them, nothing's happened since then. People kept waiting. Then gasoline tankers started rolling out of here every day and there didn't seem to be any more money. That went on for a couple of years until, at a tribal meeting, this representative from the Uncle Sam Petroleum Company said there wasn't any money in our wells, in the Big Cypress wells anyway, and that the oil in those wells was what they called "waste oil." Nobody knew what waste oil was, but we knew it meant there wasn't going to be any money in it, because the one thing that was clear was that there was something nobody was saying, and you couldn't get the Tribal Council to think there was anything wrong with it. That was a low time, a low time amidst a long time of low time. It takes awhile to know you're being cheated, and sometimes it's too late.

There was one election when somebody caught wind of the fact that Chief Billy had mailing lists nobody else had. You didn't have to live on the Reservation to vote; you just had to be on the tribal register, and there were people on the register living all over. It's just that nobody knew where they were, or who they were sometimes, except Chief Billy.

One of the daughters of John Goins, June Goins, stood up in a tribal meeting bringing up the fact that there weren't any records of how people living off the Reservation had voted—no charter of names or who they'd voted for. June's father was thinking of running for chief of the tribe and everybody knew it. "What is it you want, June?" Chief Billy had said, ruffled, but not like he'd done anything wrong, but like June was a pain in the ass, and he was going to show everybody how willing he was to hear out even the most unreasonable request.

"I want every name of everybody who's on the tribal register and where they live, and when it comes election day I want to see a signed ballot with the stamp of a notary public on anybody who does a mail-in vote."

Chief Billy lifted his head and flashed that grin of his, like he was mopping up somebody else's spilt milk and wasn't he a good Presbyterian for doing it.

"Fine!" he said. "Consider it done."

That summer somebody started setting fire to people's houses. Nobody knew for sure who was burning down the houses but some said Chief Billy was behind it, that his thugs, most of them tribal cops, were going around finding out who was home and who wasn't. It's easier to burn down somebody's house when they're not home. Four or five houses burned down in two weeks, and none of those people would have voted for him, and one of them was a son of John Goins.

It got so hardly anybody would stir out of their house. Just when it seemed everybody was sure it was Chief Billy doing it, a house one of his nephews was living in burned down. I think maybe Chief Billy even owned it. So people stopped saying it was Chief Billy who was having people's houses burned down, because he wouldn't have set fire to one of his own houses. The way he did things though, he got people not knowing what to think, got you to thinking you were just being distrustful. No one ever did find out who was burning down the houses. It stopped about a week before tribal elections.

Anybody living off the Reservation had to have their vote in by the day of the election, and June Goins, Frank Goins and Sylvie Mayfair were down at the Infirmary counting the votes of everybody who'd mailed in their ballot. Those were the last votes counted. Chief Billy Farmer won again and nobody was sure how that happened, with so many people not wanting him to be chief anymore. I knew he was ticked off because so many people didn't want him to be chief, saw the smoke of that, and where most people would just go ahead and not be chief when so many people didn't want you to, Chief Billy was okay with it. He was a Presbyterian after all. I thought maybe his wanting to be chief came from that, or he had his own reasons for wanting to be chief, but no matter what he did, it didn't seem to bother him, except he died of a heart attack forty years later. But that could happen to most anybody.

Thomas Matoas Paint was like a bear, round and fat and strong, had two ponytails and always wore the same blue polyester shirt and a pair of blue jeans. Thomas was the one who first time took me up on the Mountain. People called it "going up on the House," because the Sacred Mountain is the house to the four thunder beings. Me and Thomas are riding down the road, and he's talking away, driving that old '59 Rambler of his, and telling me the most serious things in the world. That Rambler station wagon had wooden sides, and so much play in the steering wheel you had to keep turning left and right just to go straight, and the gear shift would come out in your hand sometimes when you were shifting gears and you'd have to put it back in while you were driving down the road.

"Warren, you're giving away all your power," he says, driving down the road, turning that steering wheel back and forth. "The trouble with you is you tell everybody everything you know. You're giving away all your power. You don't have to tell anybody anything."

I didn't know if he was kidding or just trying to get my goat. Thomas could do that sometimes. He could bait you and then watch you with that twinkle in his eyes, watch what you'd do.

"Okay, Thomas, how is it I tell too much?"

"In your head! People can see you talking to

yourself all the time, inside your head!" he said. "They don't even know how they know it, but it's how they know you, as someone who's talking and telling about themselves all the time in their head. 'I'm alright or I'm not alright; I'm alright, I'm not alright.' You got Owl medicine. Why don't you use it?"

So Thomas Matoas Paint drove me up on the Mountain in his old Rambler station wagon. All I had was a blanket and a medicine bundle. Thomas said I had to have a medicine bundle. But Thomas had all sorts of stuff: a tent, cans of food, a couple of six-packs, a radio.

"Who knows, up here we might get a Twins game or something," he said.

We drove up over Whitetop and through the Kanawche Valley. There was a dirt road to the foot of the Mountain but there weren't any roads on the Mountain. You didn't go to the top anyway. Everybody who went up on the Mountain camped on the side of the Mountain somewhere. That first time, when we had found a good spot where Thomas Matoas Paint wanted to camp, I started heading up the trail.

"If I don't see you on the fourth day I'll come up and gather your bones," he said with that twinkle in his eye. Hell, there were mountain lions all through the Seven Mountains.

I went up on the House and didn't eat anything for three days. While I was up there I had a dream, a vision. I dreamed Aunt Ida came to me, except it wasn't Aunt Ida. She was younger and she wasn't wearing those old blue jeans and boots. I'd never seen her young before, but that's who she was. She was wearing calfskin leather and her hair was tied back in the traditional way. She came out of a fog cloud in the morning, when the mist lay thick on the Mountain. She didn't say anything, she didn't say, "How are you doing, Warren? When are you going to come visit me?" She held out her hand and she's got dark blue berries of cedar there. She hands them to me and I take them. I couldn't wake up since I wasn't dreaming, and when I came down from the Mountain I brought some of those cedar berries with me.

"That's good, Warren," Thomas said to me. "That's a start; you found a tree ally, and you found a treatment for Koosie Youngblood's diabetes." We boiled them up in a pot and strained them for Koosie. We did it right there in her house where she could watch. I still hang cedar bundles in my house, and when I feel like someone's energy has invaded mine, I use cedar smoke to purify.

Thomas Matoas Paint was the one who told me about how a separate reality, a suppressed past embedded in the world as we see it, can arise into the events of the present. He said that whenever anything happens that could be called coincidence, you should look around at every detail of the trees and the rocks and sky, because that moment is meant to tell you something. He said it matters if you acknowledge it. It matters because there is a message from the spirit world.

Thomas Matoas Paint was like the ambassador Indian; he talked to everybody, white people even, anybody who would *listen*. Most white people don't want to listen, they just want to talk, and there were a lot of Indians who didn't want to listen to Thomas Matoas Paint because what he said was pretty much true. There was white smoke to him and most people just don't want to talk about the truth, not on the Reservation anyway. There was enough truth all around us and nobody wanted to talk about it.

Thomas had what he called his little government bungalow. It had faded brown siding and a couple of iron pots, with something like big mums growing in them, set out on each side of the door. But Thomas didn't actually live there in that government bungalow; he just kept his stuff there. Thomas had built a teepee out of newspaper and cardboard and sprayed it all over with shellac and paint.

"No Uwharrie ever lived in no teepee," Gene Middle Dawn told him.

"I know that," Thomas said. "But no Uwharrie ever had a transistor radio either."

He slept in the teepee, and cooked and ate his food in the teepee. He would sit in there on his big butt on the dirt floor on a pillow, or naked sometimes because it could be so hot, and he'd pull out his pipe, or clean his jewelry, or read a book. He was all the time reading books, sprawled out on his bed, a little homemade job that sat just about six inches off the ground with a foam rubber pad covered with a Navaho blanket. I think his mother was Navaho or something.

He had painted pictures all over the outside of his teepee. There was a big red arm and a horse with an Indian rider, but mostly there were words in red and black letters all over it. There were a lot of Indian names there in big letters—Tecumseh, Dennis Banks, Russell Means, Crazy Horse, Ira Hayes—and some others, and some things like "AIM HIGH" and "WALK THE RED ROAD." On the inside there was stuff written in ink pen, quotes and things, and bits of philosophy.

Thomas had his teepee and then one day he just torched it.

"Next time I'll put all the writing on the outside," Thomas said, but he never did make another paper-maché teepee. That was it. He moved a bunch of his stuff out to his little government bungalow and burned the teepee. He hated the bungalow and for five or six months he lived under a blue tarp.

Thomas had what the Kowache would call "an attitude," but that's not what it was really. He told me about a time when he was working on a road crew and saw a Kowache man taking a dump behind a tree. Thomas snuck up behind him, shook the bushes and growled like a bear. He said that white man came out of those bushes running so fast he never thought

about how his pants were down around his knees
until he fell flat on his face going downhill. The man
kept falling and trying to pull his pants up and run at
the same time, with a big hunk of toilet paper in his
hand.

I laughed when he told me that, but I said,
"Thomas, you could've got yourself killed doing
something like that to a Kowache man."

"Maybe I could," he said. "But that man was a
real asshole."

Thomas Matoas Paint was a real human being;
not everybody is. He was one authentic Indian. He
made it his life mission to be an Indian; not everybody has the heart to do that anymore. He was like a
one-man tribe, and you can't be an Indian without a
tribe, so he went around trying to recruit Indians to
be themselves, to be authentic human beings. We'd be
shooting pool at the Legion Hall and Thomas'd be
giving us the history of the Indian peoples, with a
Budweiser in his hand. He was religious, with or without a beer in his hand.

"White lies are still the cause of the greatest suffering in the world. Prosperity, at the expense of
another people, at the expense of the land, of the
Earth is ultimately a lie. Providing comfort and security for one people while devastating Mother Earth is
a lie. Temporarily it can serve as truth but there's no
way it can last. It's founded upon the suffering and
deprivation of life."

Thomas Matoas Paint could get worked up into

his "oratory," as he called it. Maybe Gettis, or Joe Bad Crow, or me, or somebody was trying to take a shot, but you couldn't do that when Thomas was worked up into his oratory. The pool game would come to a stop and we'd all stand around, sip on beers, and listen to Thomas Matoas Paint. You can only do one meaningful thing at a time.

"We see the evidence in oil wells, automobile manufacturing, chemical compounds, logging operations, road building; the devastation of life on land and life in the oceans for the benefit of a single people. For a time, it might seem like the increase of food, clothing and housing are good things, easy travelling on super highways, hospital medicine. But what's the cost? What's the real quality of life? What are the *real* consequences of so-called improvements? Isn't the destruction of the life systems of the Earth a direct descendant of the practices and policies set forth against the Indian peoples of this country? It's still happening. Truth doesn't go away because one people have a bigger army than another. Truth is bigger than that, and lasts far longer than a lifetime."

One night we were sitting in this bar in Jackson, listening to a jukebox and drinking a beer. We'd thought we were going to a powwow and showed up at the Infirmary but we had the wrong weekend and so we'd gone into town.

Thomas was wearing that short-sleeved blue knit shirt of his, must've had a whole drawer full of them because he never wore any other shirt or ever wore a coat. "Not all these people are alive," he said. "Some of them are dead. They're ghosts! Look at them. It's pretty easy to tell if you look in their eyes, but you can see it if you squint your eyes too!"

I thought he was joking because Thomas *would* do that kind of thing. I tried though, squinting at a group of young white guys at the bar, telling stories about each other.

Thomas was amused at me squinting at those white guys but he put his big hand on my arm affectionately. I guess he was afraid he'd hurt my feelings and was sorry for making fun of me.

"I don't mean to laugh, but don't try so hard. You look like you're taking a crap."

I felt silly, but I tried it again.

"Good!" he said. "Now how many of those men are dead?"

"Three?" I said.

"Good," he said. "If you ever got into a fight with them you would just focus all your energy on that one guy who's alive. You beat him and all the rest of them will run. They're afraid because they're not authentic human beings. Very few white people are. They're just good at self-promotion. But it's here where we make the world better," and he tapped his chest with the four fingers of his left hand.

"It's what is in here that's important. It's what we *feel*. It isn't even what we think. There's not time for anything but being authentic, being a real human being. If you compare yourself to anyone, think that you are better than someone else, that your truth is better than their truth, it eventually leads to suffering. Believing their truth is better than your truth, that too will lead to suffering."

Thomas Matoas Paint said he was a medicine man in training but I think he *was* a medicine man. I took Ruby Keehoe, my sister, to see Thomas Matoas Paint when she was having shoulder pain and pain in her upper chest. He was living in that government cinder-block house and Ruby was sitting at what he called his kitchen table, except Thomas never ate at his kitchen table. There were bones and feathers and crystals all over it. He passed over her arm several times with a large clear white crystal and got a funny expression on his face. He was sniffing the air.

"Do you smell something, Warren?" he asked me. I was just sitting there watching.

I sniffed, "Yeah, I smell cigarette smoke." You know, stale cigarette smoke like in a bar or in an old hotel room.

"Yeah! That's it. That's what it is. Old stale cigarette smoke," Thomas said. "Ruby, do you smoke?"

"No," she said. "I don't smoke."

Thomas Matoas Paint was puzzled and he kept passing that crystal over Ruby's arm and up by her shoulder, like he was working on some energy or something stuck in inside her arm. Then he stopped and looked at her face real close.

"Did you used to smoke?"

"Well, I used to smoke," Ruby said. "When I was

at Brigham Young I started smoking a little, and me and Sun Susie used to smoke together."

"A little? You used to smoke a lot, Ruby," I said. "A couple packs a day anyway. What was that, Camels?"

She gave me a look that would send a lizard under a rock. "No," she said. "Marlboro."

"That's it. I thought so," Thomas Matoas Paint said. "The poison is working its way out. That's why we're smelling old smoke. Your arm's going to get better."

It did, too. Thomas could do that stuff where most people can't focus enough to make something like that happen.

"A wise man knows what makes anything sacred," Thomas Matoas Paint always said. He healed with crystals, but he told me once you could heal with a Colgate toothbrush if you believed you could.

After Sun Susie disappeared Thomas Matoas Paint told me she had been coming to him and that he was treating her for depression. He was making packs of herbs for her. A lot of people thought it was suicide but he didn't think so.

It was Thomas Matoas Paint who told me the truth about Knud Guunegai, as much truth as you could know. We were sitting in his Rambler one day when he told me about Knud Guunegai. Thomas liked to package his herbs and sell them to people sitting in the front seat of his Rambler, so there we were. He had a long look in his eye, like the blue in the mountains. He had a plastic bag on his lap because we were bagging some nettles. I knew he had something to say because he'd stopped bagging those nettles.

"You know, Warren," he said, "the Kowache never were looking for uranium, not really."

"But they found uranium."

"Maybe they did, but what they found wasn't any good," Thomas said. "What they really wanted was the oil. They didn't know how much oil there was. Now they know. Chief Billy had those white guys here from the Army Corps of Engineers talking about uranium, and they dug some pits, and buried them back up. But they were never interested in uranium. They knew there was oil here."

"What are you talking about?"

"The uranium was just an excuse," he said. "They couldn't just come on the Reservation and start looking all over for oil, and so they say they're looking for uranium. They call it a matter of national security. And they didn't just go on some land. They went all over, over on the Kettle, the *Urapitan*, Kachawna Basin. What do you think all those yellow trucks were, the ones with the little man with a drop for a head and wearing a hard hat painted on the side doors? Those weren't army trucks or any kind of government truck. Those were the trucks of some big-time oil company, contracted by them anyway, to find oil. It was probably Esso or Pure, Standard, or somebody like that. Chief Billy goes into his bullshit about jobs and royalties. Lewis Martin got himself a brand-new pick-up truck and Star Bad Boy paved his driveway. Next thing you know Chief Billy builds himself a new house. They knew it was here; they just didn't know how much or how good it was. Knud knew and ended up dead in a ditch down by the river."

"Knud Guunegai was just a falling-down drunk."

"Didn't Hanay Rose look into that allotment business over in the Kachawna Basin? Somebody thought there was oil over there. Maybe they were just waiting until the oil prices went up, and then the ones who've got the mineral rights are sitting on a gold mine. Knud knew they were looking for oil. You remember that story he was always telling everybody about how he could witch for oil with a piece of stick. He was hanging around Gannon's Motel and Trading Post telling every white man he saw how he could dowse for oil."

"You're saying that oil got him killed?"

"You figure it out. Did it ever make sense that Knud Guunegai turned up dead where he did?"

There were people saying Sun Susie had been depressed, and I guess that was true, and so people were guessing suicide. There was plenty of that on the Reservation, and shortly after Sun Susie disappeared, her purse, identification card and shoes were found on the side of Highway 10, so everybody said, "There it is. Suicide."

The police were going to give up the investigation but then Ruay Overmoon found an abandoned van over behind Old Man's Back. The side was bashed in. The van had several of Sun Susie's belongings in it. She had gone to the AIM rally and never made it home and they found a comb, her coat and a cosmetics case. The van was white, a Chevy with California plates, and when they traced it to Los Angeles it turned out the guy who owned the van had reported it stolen about a month before any of this had happened.

My sister said she was going to find out what had happened to Sun Susie because they were good friends. They were good friends even before Ruby got that job at the Presbyterian Hospital, though I guess Sun Susie was probably five or six years older than Ruby.

There was some part of Ruby that didn't trust other people to do what they said, and this included the tribal police. She would say, "If you want something done right you do it yourself." I thought maybe she had learned that in college but she said her foster mother, Barbara Keehoe, had taught her that.

"You know Sun Susie, Warren. She was going to the rally. Does that sound like suicide? She was getting that horse of hers ready for that race over in Lansdale. Sun Susie didn't commit suicide."

Ruby was already working three jobs: one at the hospital, another doing the books for some welding company, and another working at the liquor store on weekends. And she was raising Anthony John and not getting much help from Joe Bad Crow. They were fighting, or if they weren't fighting, they weren't talking, not to each other anyway.

They weren't living on the Reservation at that time and Joe was working as a carpenter's helper. The Kowache were building a lot of houses down by the river. He and Ruby would fight one night and Joe'd leave out early the next morning, go work a little while, and some time in the afternoon knock off work and go to a bar just so he wouldn't have to go back home. And that just pissed Ruby off even more.

Maybe Ruby was frustrated because she wasn't a lawyer, or maybe she never wanted to be or didn't know why she went to college. She was working in the hospital, and her best friend was murdered, and she was convinced the police weren't doing anything, not the county police or the tribal police.

Then a road worker found a fresh dug grave-shaped pit out at Raven's Rock County Park, and word was it was meant for Sun Susie. Maybe the gravedigger had been disturbed or he decided it was too close to the road, but they found some lipstick out in the parking lot there and Ruby caught wind of it, heard about the lipstick and found out it was Revlon # 22 or something, the same kind Sun Susie used. Ruby knew that kind of thing because Sun Susie was her best friend.

We rode out to Raven's Rock Park during Ruby's lunch break. Driving into the park we came across a road crew and Ruby rolled down the window and asked them where the gravesite was, the same as if she was a county coroner or something. She had that way, even being Indian. The guy told her right where the grave pit was, and she thanked him just like she was a county official or something.

The grave pit wasn't marked off; I think they were just going to fill it back in. It wasn't much but it was a grave alright, and called up that feeling that if we found Sun Susie, she wasn't going to be alive. It was shallow, but there was something about that pit, and not like whoever had dug it was going to dump a load of oil illegally and cover it up. It wasn't that kind of feeling. We just drove back to the hospital in silence.

I didn't ever fully understand what was between Sun Susie and her real mother. Ruby had told me they never spoke to each other, that if they ran into each other in the laundromat one of them would just walk around the other way, not even looking at each other. Ruby said Sun Susie told her it had to do with Sun Susie's dad. But it was more than that. Sun Susie's dad was dead, so some things weren't going to change. He killed himself by drinking, that was all that was said. I don't know if it was liver or diabetes or something else, but he killed himself by drinking.

But it was only a couple of days after me and Ruby had gone out to that grave pit that Sun Susie's mother told Ruby that if she wanted anything of value she needed to go through Sun Susie's house and get it out. She knew my sister and Sun Susie were close and she respected that. This is the kind of thing that keeps people together, even in bad times. But they were going to burn down that house.

Sun Susie's mother's way of looking at things wasn't that unusual on the Reservation. Many Uwharrie families are divided, and it usually comes down to some of the family being Indian and some of the family being Presbyterian and preferring the white ways. Two of Sun Susie's aunts had married white men and moved as far away from the Reservation as they could, and one of Sun Susie's cousins was a fanatic who had always kept trying to convince Sun Susie to move to Chicago because there were so many "eligible Christian brothers" there.

And then there was Sun Susie's mother; she was a traditional. Sun Susie was caught in between two worlds, but what complicated things even more for Sun Susie, though it was never mentioned, was that Sun Susie's mother was not the biological daughter of Gary Yellow Knife, the man Sun Susie knew as her grandfather. Nobody really knew who Sun Susie's mother's father was, but it was commonly thought he might be white. Sun Susie's mother, besides being traditional, was as inflexible as can be, which is why she wanted to burn down Sun Susie's house. It became clear when Ruby and me met Sun Susie's uncle outside the house, that anything taken out of the house could only be those things made by Uwharrie hands. Everything else was to be burned along with the house, and that meant a perfectly good TV and a sofa. And any picture had to be taken out of its picture frame. I don't know why a picture wasn't considered to be from the white man's world, but Hanay Rose, he was Sun Susie's uncle, said it was alright.

Hanay Rose was a little man, never got old just kept getting shorter, and he wasn't exactly a traditional. He'd worked on the railroad when there was a railroad, and he'd been in World War I, and it was always with him, always a part of who he was. Hanay Rose kept his hair cropped like a white soldier. He always wore long sleeves and always tucked his shirt in, no matter how hot it was, and he never wore a hat because our people didn't traditionally wear hats. He said hats made you bald like an old white man. He was kind of a mixed bag. I asked him how it was that he worked for the railroad and he just said that it was something he did when he was young and didn't know any better. When he cooked it was with clay pots, and he ate out of a clay bowl just like Sun

Susie's mother.

Hanay Rose sat down in a chair and started looking through a magazine, like he was ready to burn the whole house down without worrying about what was in there, said something about the police having already been there, but we knew that. They had come a day or two before and filed a report which said about as much as they'd found nothing.

I noticed the paper coffee cup with some coffee still in the bottom of it that hadn't dried out, and peanut shells on the floor, but I didn't think anything of it at first.

"There was a man here," Ruby said, and just the thought of it seemed to make her angry. I knew; she was my sister. When something was building it drew up dark like a storm. I watched, waiting for something, like the wind and the rain. I knew it was there. She scowled. Maybe she and Sun Susie had spent some long, dark nights drinking beer and dreaming about getting married, having a good husband and having children. It hadn't worked out for either of them in some funny kind of way because here Sun Susie was probably dead, and I knew things were going bad to worse between her and Joe. Ruby scowled.

Well, the fact that there had been a man there made sense to me; there were peanut shells on the floor, but I figured it was just the kind of thing the police out of Jackson would do: come into a missing woman's house and leave all sorts of their shit around.

I looked over at Hanay Rose and he had stopped flipping through that magazine.

There were three cardboard boxes full of books up against the wall. Ruby had already looked at that, and looked into the refrigerator for what kind of food was in there, just like the police had probably done. There was a small desk there, and the top drawer was slightly open. Maybe the police opened that drawer. Maybe they had left it slightly open like that. Ruby was looking at a horoscope cut out of the newspaper and taped to the refrigerator, and suddenly I understood—and I couldn't say why I did—I knew someone had looked through those boxes of books and that it might not have been the police. It was just one coffee cup, and there were those peanut shells on the floor.

I went over to the boxes of books and there on the top was a book of crossword puzzles, you know, one of those Dell books you can pick up cheap for thirty-five cents. I looked at it, and inside of it, just like it was meant to be there, was a piece of three-hole notebook paper torn in half. It would have been easy not to have seen it, to have thought it was somebody's doodling paper working out a cross-word, or maybe not have known what it meant. It was almost nothing, except there were three names written in a short column, written in a light script with a # 3 pencil:

Knud Guunegai
Margaret Brown
Sam Brown

That was all, but when I saw Knud Guunegai's name written down like that, I couldn't help but think about what Thomas Matoas Paint had said about Knud Guunegai. I knew my sister wouldn't have known about the allotment business; she'd been away at college then, I think, or was living with that guy she thought she was going to marry in Utah.

Ruby took down the horoscope Sun Susie had cut out and taped to the refrigerator. She read it, shaking her head, like that horoscope might say, "Don't go out drinking Friday night."

"This isn't right," Ruby said, and her jaws almost locked up. "Sun Susie's cut out a horoscope that's not even hers and stuck it on the refrigerator."

"How's that?" I said.

"She's not an Aries."

"Must be a boyfriend," I said without thinking. "But this here is strange. There's a little piece of paper here and it's got Margaret Brown's name on it and her son Sam Brown, and Knud Guunegai."

"So who are those people, Margaret Brown and Sam Brown?"

"You remember them. They lived over in the Kachawna Basin. Margaret was a traditional, raised goats and sheep, but still, she made sure Sam got an education. He lived off the Reservation for awhile, but came back and lived with her, helped out raising the goats."

I didn't know for sure why Knud Guunegai's name would be on a scrap of paper in Sun Susie's house, or Margaret and Sam Brown's either, but I was beginning to get some idea. Everybody more or less knew that whole mess about oil in the Kachawna never happened in the right way, and the Tribal Council sat on their hands and looked the other way, leaving it to our Chapter House, a society and nothing to do with government, to try to figure out what was going on wrong. Hanay Rose tried, but nobody ever did figure that mess out—not really.

My sister didn't know the story about the allotment business, how back in the twenties, as a way of working its way onto Indian lands, the federal government had come up with this thing called allotments, which meant that Reservation land was subdivided, and everybody had been given 160 acres held in trust by the BIA, the Bureau of Indian Affairs. It was the U.S. government's way of getting back the oil they didn't know they'd given away when they put us on the Reservation. An allottee could sell that land or they could lease it. And when they opened up the oil wells in the Kachawna Basin, I think Ruby was away living with her foster family. Some people were for oil wells anyway; thought it was a good thing we had the oil wells, said they gave people jobs, and people needed a job to feel good about themselves. The BIA told people they could get money for their land without giving up their land. Now how does that work? It was mostly old people they told this too, and old people need money. It was a lease for a year; the people could keep right on living on their land. They all got slips of paper with account numbers on them and were told that in a month's time they could go get money for their land.

All that mess with the allotments happened because of a white man named Gordon Gannon. Nobody ever did figure out that mess, except Gordon Gannon was some kind of smoke screen for some of the crookedest crap you ever saw. You couldn't make up that kind of stuff.

Gordon Gannon was a white businessman, a middleman, who lived down on Highway 10, and a sometimes friend of Chief Billy. He was the workingest man I ever saw; he had the white man's disease. Grandmother always said he was one of those white people who made out like he had more money than he did, but I thought it was the other way around, that Gordon Gannon had more money than he said, one of those who is never rich enough, no matter how much money they made. He ran a Buick dealership, and a realty company in Brownsville, and owned a motel and a trading post, and was an all-around land speculator. The wheels were always turning. The story was that Gordon Gannon's house, down on Highway 10 after leaving the New Reservation, was designed by Frank Lloyd Wright. It was a brick ranch with a Hercules fence and a swimming pool. A couple of white boys snuck in there once at night, to go swimming in that pool, and drowned. There was a lawsuit and Gordon Gannon had to pay out money to the families of those boys, and put up that chain-link fence around his pool, with barbed wire around the top. That's the story I heard of why Gordon Gannon had a fence around his swimming pool.

He was short for a white man, muscular, with a square jaw and face. Out and about he was always dressed up, coat and tie, so he'd look like a real businessman instead of a snake in the grass, but out in his yard he just wore a tee shirt, a white tee shirt. If he wasn't at his car dealership or his realty company, he'd be working in his yard. He'd be out there watering his yard, or he'd have a shovel or a grubbing hoe in his hand, looking like a simple man, in his white tee shirt, washing off his fancy white Buick with a hose from the well. He was always doing something.

When I was a kid Gannon's motel had been called Bob's Hotel. Ruay Overmoon told the story of how this guy named Bob stood up at a Tribal Council meeting, all bent out of shape, because he couldn't have his hotel because it was on tribal land. Somebody had worked out some kind of way, and Bob said it wasn't him, that for twenty years everybody thought Bob's hotel was sitting off the Reservation. I guess it could have worked out all right but nobody liked Bob.

"This is my hotel," he said, and Ruay Overmoon did a different voice. "It was left to me and I won't have you taking everything away from me either. This is my hotel. All these years I've taken good care of it. I've scrubbed the floors and stoked the fires and I've painted the walls. I've waited on the guests and cooked for them and made the beds. It's mine! Do you think I'll let you take it away from me? I don't owe you anything. That's all I've got to say."

Then Bob's wife got up. She was really the one who had scrubbed the floors and stoked the fires and painted the walls and waited on the guests and cooked for them, but she got up and she was hotter than he was, and called us Indian givers and all that shit, talking about how ungrateful we were and how she had fed Indians from the back of her hotel when they were starving, and where were all the tourists going to stay who wanted to buy our "trinkets." And then all their relatives and neighbors came parading up and they spoke too. The room was packed full of white people who had stayed at that hotel, and every one of them got up and talked about how great the hotel was.

The funny thing was Ruay Overmoon had heard it that Joyce Red Horse, who was on the Tribal Council then, was trying to get it so the tribe could buy the hotel, except Bob wouldn't sell. Then, when the Tribal Council said Bob and his wife could stay in their hotel and keep it as long as they lived, he turned around and sold it to Gordon Gannon. Ruay

Overmoon said Bob and his wife went off to Las Vegas or something.

The whole thing ended up back in front of the Tribal Council, and Gordon Gannon was saying the tribe couldn't take away his hotel because he had just invested all this money in it and that would be undue hardship. Joyce Red Horse was still trying to get it so the tribe would buy the hotel, but Gordon Gannon was asking way too much for that rattrap of a hotel. They let the hotel stay. Gordon Gannon took out a whole lot of insurance on Bob's Hotel, and sure enough, within a month, the hotel burned to the ground. Nobody really knows who did it. Some say it was Indians, and some say Gannon did it himself. I don't know, never did find out. But Gannon built the hotel back, but he called it a motel and it had a trading post with it, just like the old one.

Somehow, along with that hotel and the Poison Creek Store, Gordon Gannon owned land along the river north, in the Kachawna Basin. His land in the Kachawna Basin bordered the Reservation. There was a barbed-wire fence on cedar posts marking where Gordon Gannon's land ended and where the Reservation began. Gordon Gannon knew all about the allotments and he had his own way of getting 160 acres. Every couple of months he would have those cedar posts pulled up and the fence moved further onto Margaret Brown's land or Hahay Charlie's land—reservation land—sometimes as much as two or three hundred feet. Hired hands worked at night, and Gordon Gannon would always wait a couple of months before he had the fences moved again.

When I was a kid, Grandfather, Joe Bad Crow's uncle Sammy Greys, Ross Rose, and Hanay Rose and some others would take shovels, hammers and nails and go move the fences part way back, but Chief Billy said they couldn't do that. There was a lot of talk about how nothing could be done about it because of Gordon Gannon being a white man with a lot of money. This went on for a long time, and it wasn't too hard to figure out: Chief Billy Farmer had himself a Buick Le Sabre, and there's no telling what kind of deal he had gotten on it. That Buick, or his pick-up truck, would be parked in town because Chief Billy was having lunch with Gordon Gannon.

Eventually Hanay Rose and some others got up money for a lawyer. It happened around our kitchen table: Grandfather, Mom, Aunt Ida and I think maybe Sun Susie, who was living off the Reservation then, Claris Locklear, whose son got killed in Vietnam, Joe's father, Ruay Overmoon, Guthern Young Bear and some others. They took it to court. That was something that didn't happen too often, because it was like throwing your money away if you did. Chief Billy made sure we never said it was an official Uwharrie case; he didn't want it to reflect badly on the tribe.

A young lawyer named Robert Unlai represented our Chapter House in civil court. They practiced their testimonies around our kitchen table. Robert

Unlai wasn't Uwharrie; he was Lakota and had represented other tribes when it came to land issues. He had his hair slicked down like they did in the city and smelled like soap. Robert Unlai was polite and didn't sit down until Grandmother made him sit down. He had a briefcase. I had never seen an Indian with a briefcase before.

Everybody listened to Robert Unlai. I guess everybody knew Robert Unlai was one smart Indian because he'd been to Yale. He said he knew of a lot of ways white people got land from Indian tribes but he'd never seen anything like this. They all got to talking about why a Kowache with as much money as Gordon Gannon would be pilfering land.

"Well, I don't think he does have so much money," Grandmother said. "I think if he didn't have a Buick dealership he wouldn't have a Buick, and he's so proud that he's got it, that he washes it all the time."

I'd heard all that at dinner ever since I could remember, and all that talk of why Gordon Gannon was going after Indian land. I just figured it was all because he had the white man's disease: wanting to want things.

Somebody said something about drillers and trucks on the New Reservation. The New Reservation is bigger than the Old Reservation, and was a concession of land the Kowache gave back to us when their gold mines panned out in the Kachawna Basin back in the 1800s. When they thought it was wasted land they gave it back to us.

There had been occasional drillers on the New Reservation, and big trucks, when the government was looking for uranium. The drillers had made rough roads, and the roads washed out into gullies, and before the rains came white men hauled the wood out, sold it in town for ten dollars a cord. That was wood people depended on because we had wood-burning stoves; a lot of us didn't have electricity then.

Chief Billy Farmer said that the federal government had rights to that land because of the uranium, but those Kowache cutting that wood weren't with the federal government. Chief Billy never did do anything about that.

"Do you think there's uranium on your Reservation?" Robert Unlai asked us.

"What is uranium?" Grandfather asked.

"It's a mineral," Ruay Overmoon said. "The U.S. government needs it to make bombs because the Russians have got bombs."

"There's no uranium on this land. Whoever thought there was uranium here anyway?" It was David Greys who said this.

"What do you think all those white trucks with the little light bulb man with a lightning bolt around his head are about?" Hanay Rose said. "Those are uranium trucks. When the U.S. government says they want to look for uranium they can come right here on the Reservation; it's a matter of 'national security.'"

Robert Unlai told us about other tribes opposing government contracts concerning uranium, oil, molybdenum, whatever. It always came down to the same thing: the U.S. government didn't make a bad deal for itself. They were always ready to use something, use the land, people, whatever. The Navahos never would have ended up sitting on a uranium mine if Einstein hadn't come along, and there wouldn't be Indians dying of cancer and radiation sickness from tailings, contaminated groundwater and from working in the mines. We knew about that, and there weren't too many people who were happy about the idea of uranium being dug out of here. But there were always some who were for it, even knowing those things, because there is so much poverty on the Reservation.

Hanay Rose told about Knud Guunegai taking samples of uranium from one white man and showing them to another, and getting a cigar and a bottle of whiskey out of it, and Aunt Ida said something about the holes the drillers were leaving on the land on the New Reservation.

"They're filling up those holes with hard mud, but they don't fence in the holes, and chickens, goats and cows are falling in there and can't get out. You ought to see Mae Cole Rattler's land; it's like a cement floor!"

"Benthonite," Robert Unlai said.

"What's benthonite?" Hanay Rose asked.

Benthonite was the substance they used to fill the

pits after the holes were drilled. The idea was that if they didn't find what they were looking for they could fill in the pit and the land could be reclaimed. They classified it as clay but it was more like granite.

"I saw one of Mae Cole Rattler's cows with her arms and legs sticking out," Aunt Ida said. "There wasn't anything you could do to get her out. She was dead."

"What's Chief Billy Farmer say to you about this?" Robert Unlai asked us.

"I don't think Chief Billy knows about this," somebody said, and somebody else said he did.

Finally David Greys said, "Mr. Unlai, you say we can win this case. How much do we owe you if we do and how much do we owe you if we don't?"

"You pay me what you can," he said. He knew how to talk with Grandfather and Grandmother and the others. He knew they'd pay him well, more than they could afford. They knew it took money to walk into the white man's courtroom.

It did come to trial and we won. That surprised everybody, but we knew a court ruling wasn't going to stop Gordon Gannon from moving the fences again, that he could just keep doing it, and Joe's father and Hanay Rose and some others would be back moving them again.

Next thing you know *all* the fences are down, and they're putting a road in there, coming in off of County Road 1201. Suddenly there are big trucks in the Kachawna Basin and everybody's wondering what's going on and nobody seems to know. It didn't seem like anybody had asked permission, and this wasn't uranium; an oil company had just gone on to Reservation land and started drilling. Down at the county courthouse they told Aunt Ida and Hanay Rose that they should ask somebody on the Reservation, and it turned out Megal Upchurch, who had been the Chapter House secretary for twenty years, knew about a copy of a lease with the U.S. Petroleum Corporation negotiating the right to drill for oil on Reservation land. Megal Upchurch thought we all knew about it, but the lease had been approved in 1951 and the Chapter House officers didn't even know about it! Hanay Rose didn't know about it; Ruay Overmoon and Guthern Young Bear didn't know about it, and Megal Upchurch couldn't explain it. It was just a piece of paper that had been transferred to her by Chief Billy's brother-in-law, who was on the Tribal Council, saying it should be kept with the records in the Chapter House. Chief Billy's name was the first on the list to sell the oil rights.

All anybody could really figure out was that the Tribal Council had decided to sign an oil exploration lease with the Uncle Sam Petroleum Corporation. Maybe the Tribal Council wanted the money to get used here; maybe they were going to get some of that money, maybe Chief Billy and a few of his own. Almost ten thousand dollars for 800 acres or so of land. A dollar an acre! Rent for one year with four dollars minimum royalty. That was nothing for what was given up, and nobody knew if any of us would ever see one cent of that money. There were signatures on the lease, four of them: Bejjie Rose, Corlay Hathale, Jim Hathale and Hahay Charlie. It turned out none of them really knew what they were signing when they signed that lease. Jim Hathale was dead but the others were still alive.

"I didn't sign anything so they could dig in the ground," Hahay Charlie said. Her husband had gotten killed in World War II and her son and daughter had moved to the city to look for jobs. She lived alone, not even any cats and dogs to keep away witches because she kept the old ways. Hahay Charlie had kept the little slip of paper they had given her in a honeysuckle basket. The slip of paper had account numbers on it.

"Did they tell you anything when they gave you this paper?" Hanay Rose asked her.

"They said for me to go to the BIA and see if they had some money for me over there. I went over there once but I couldn't get it. What's it mean?"

It was the same with Corlay Hathale and Bejjie Rose. Neither of them really knew what it was they'd signed, but they had each signed away the underground rights to 160 acres of tribal land. They hadn't gotten their money either. This was land in the Kachawna Basin, most of which we never thought of as anybody owning. That was sacred land. But the Tribal Council did a land transfer. The Tribal Council was saying that parcels over 500 acres were

transferable, and that they were the ones to decide
things like that. That was Chief Billy and the Tribal
Council. There was over 1200 acres in all over there,
and some of it turned out to be the land of Margaret
Brown and her son, Sam Brown. Margaret Brown
was diabetic and she had died of complications. And
her son, Sam Brown, had diabetes too, and had broken his leg when he fell off his horse looking for
goats, and nobody ever found him until he was dead.
Their land had been turned over to the tribe in 1950
because they had both died a year or two before and
there weren't any direct relatives on the tribal register.
But when I was telling all of this to Ruby we didn't
know all that. Ruby found some out later, because she
started rooting then, like a bear knowing what they
know when they know why they're digging. Nothing
stops them.

This was how the oil wells opened in the
Kachawna Basin, 1957 or '58. They were called the
Big Cypress Wells. There aren't any cypress trees on
the Uwharrie Reservation, but there had been a gold
mine back in the 1800s built with big timbers hauled
in from South Carolina or Georgia, and so somebody
called it the Big Cypress mine. The oil wells got the
same name, though the Kowache foreman just called
them the Kachawna Mines, but that's not what anybody else called it. Nobody was giving a sacred name
to that, but Uwharrie men got work, and so there was
support for it. They were saying a lot of jobs were
coming and everybody was going to be happy about

that, because one thing we needed on the Reservation was money, and Chief Billy kept signing whatever he wanted to and playing innocent, making out like nobody understood him, and then he'd say what we didn't know was that the U.S. government was threatening not to renegotiate our sovereignty if we didn't sell our mineral rights.

When I was a kid Knud Guunegai was always standing down on the Reservation Road; he lived in the road. No matter how hot or how cold it was, he would be there in his old yellow ratty corduroy shirt, or if it got really hot he'd take that shirt off and go barebacked, and hold the shirt all wadded up in his hand. Knud had a pretty thin connection. If he wasn't in the road he'd be at the Legion Hall.

I don't know where Knud got his money, but he'd get his skinny self drunk and stand in the road. He'd wave his arms back and forth like something awful had happened, or call out like a crow and sling that shirt around and around his head to get people to stop. Anybody who had to go that way—and everybody did—had to listen to what he had to say that day. It usually didn't make a whole lot of sense. Funny thing was, if Grandmother was in the car, Knud wouldn't say a word. He'd get out of the way. But when she was gone, or if she wasn't in the car, if it was just Aunt Ida and me or Mom going to town for groceries and feed, we'd have to stop.

Aunt Ida drove her old black two-door Studebaker into town to get groceries and feed for the animals. There were holes in the floorboard, and in the summertime grass grew behind the seats in that car because it was black and didn't have any back windows. The cloth of the backseat, where I always had to sit, was dusty and threadbare, with holes in it where you could see the springs and watch the road go by underneath your feet through the holes in the floorboard.

Aunt Ida would always listen to Knud Guunegai for awhile when he stopped us on the road, because she was kind that way, but I'd be in that back and it'd be getting hot back there. Knud Guunegai would be leaning in on the window, talking about all kinds of birds and how he was part of the Crow society— that's what he usually talked about—and I'd be wishing for a breeze to blow up so I could get some fresh air. Aunt Ida wouldn't say much; she'd just nod her head, until finally, when she'd taken as much as she could, she'd say, "That's good. Out of the way, Knud!" Firm but gentle. "Move out of the way there," like she was telling cows to move. She'd start the car rolling and keep it rolling, slow and heavy, like she expected Knud to move, just like you'd expect cattle to move. And he always did.

But sometimes, particularly after Grandmother died, Sun Susie would go to town with us, and if she did, she'd drive. When Sun Susie saw Knud Guunegai standing in the way she'd get this smirk on her face and stop the car a couple of hundred feet away and reach up for the pack of cigarettes she kept in the sun visor. She'd light a cigarette, and tilt her head upwards the way she did, puffing out of the side of her mouth and filling the front of the car with smoke. Some people look grim when they're smoking, like life is too hard and too difficult, and they're smoking just to think about something else for awhile. But Sun Susie loved smoking. She really did. When she was young she smiled when she smoked. And she'd gun the motor in that old Studebaker and say to Aunt Ida, "If he doesn't move I'm going to run over him."

One day Sun Susie was driving and Knud Guunegai was standing in the road carrying a whisky bottle. He was holding that bottle over his head and shaking it like it was full of power.

"Today, I'll run over him!" she said as Knud Guunegai was moving towards us with that bottle over his head. "I swear it; I'm going to run over him!" I think Sun Susie said this just to annoy Aunt Ida, because Aunt Ida kept the old ways. Knud Guunegai smiled, like he could hear what Sun Susie was saying. It was his joke, I guess, because he always got out of the way, and when the car was going by he'd slap it with his hand like it was a pony. That always made Sun Susie mad and she'd look back in the mirror and say, "One day I'm going to run over you, Knud Guunegai, and then we'll see who's laughing!"

But this day, I guess Knud Guunegai forgot he had that whisky bottle in his hand, I don't even know if it had anything in it, and maybe the car did bump into him, but when I looked back out the back window through the dust, Knud Guunegai was teetering like he was about to fall face down in the road and that bottle had smashed and broken in the dust. Maybe he tried to hit the side of the car with his hand, because he fell in the road and

Sun Susie threw back her head and laughed like a horse.

Whenever we kids were walking up the road from school and saw Knud standing in the way, we'd just skirt the road, go through the woods so he wouldn't see us and give us any trouble. We were just kids and we were afraid of his craziness.

Maybe Knud was one of those warriors who had no war to fight. Maybe those who had gotten to fight in World War II were lucky, or they had gotten themselves killed and didn't come back to live on the Reservation. Maybe drinking liquor was one way some people had to let what was inside go out. I don't know, but sometimes, after my father died, we would build a fire down by the pond, and Joe Bad Crow and me, and Johnny Black Payton sometimes, would listen to Grandfather and Ruay Overmoon tell stories. Sometimes there'd be other men there too: Hanay Rose, Ruay Overmoon, Guthern Young Bear, Lester Keestrong. Sometimes there was a bottle of whisky.

I remember once Knud Guunegai showed up down at the pond when Grandfather and Ruay Overmoon were telling these stories, and he was in one bad mood. Maybe he was all pissed off because no one had invited him, but owls and crows don't agree on anything, not even the terms of death. They are mortal enemies, and don't see the world the same way. Owls go so far as to believe crows are the manifestations of their own bad moods, and should be killed when they can, because crows give them no peace and search them out and mob them in the day-time. Crows say something equally strange.

I thought Knud Guunegai was going to fall into the fire because he wasn't paying any attention to it, like a dog can singe their hair when they don't know what a fire is. Knud had skinny little legs and I thought he was going to topple right on in, looking up into the sky and trying to point to the stars or something, and carrying on about how everything was messed up. It was like if he kept talking long enough everything would be alright—except he wasn't paying any attention to the fire. I saw Grandfather and Hanay Rose putting their hands up so Knud wouldn't fall in and burn himself up, except he was mad at them too and pushed them away.

There was a whisky bottle there, I think there was, or maybe he brought it with him, but he was looking up into the sky and shouting and pointing and carrying on, holding a whisky bottle up over his head, with a couple of men grabbing for it. He stumbled and the whisky bottle went flying into the fire. Knud Guunegai cackled like a crow, like maybe he thought the bottle was empty. It was a crazy thing and a wonder nobody got hit by broken glass. The bottle shattered and the fire flared up. Things broke up after that.

I told Aunt Ida about it the next day, and I asked her if Knud Guunegai was crazy. Aunt Ida said, "Ain't nobody crazy, Warren."

Maybe Knud Guunegai wasn't crazy but he was

sure imbalanced. For one thing he hung around with white people, and maybe that made him crazy. Aunt Ida wasn't sure that white people couldn't be crazy, and Knud Guunegai hung around a lot with this seedy old white man named O. T. Beldon. He was a drunk too, who lived down by the river under a piece of tin.

Knud Guunegai would take archeologists to look for bones, old dinosaur bones. The archeologists would show up from time to time to dig on a village site, or to get some kind of dinosaur bone they needed for some exhibit they were having, but they had to get tribal permission to do that. It wasn't that hard to do because Chief Billy was big into what he called "public relations," and there was always money in it somehow. The archeologists had figured out that the best way to get artifacts or bones, or whatever they wanted, was to give a little cornmeal to a Presbyterian convert or a bottle of whisky to Knud Guunegai. Knud would take anybody anywhere they wanted to go for a bottle of whisky, and if he didn't know where to go, he'd make it up. Making it up was mostly what he did so I guess that's why he never got into real trouble with the Council.

Knud Guunegai had this story too about dowsing for gasoline and oil. He told people that his grandmother had taught him how to do that, that it was an old Uwharrie custom, that he and his family had known for years how to find water, oil, natural gas, anything you wanted to find, with an old witchety stick. No Uwharrie ever did that.

Knud Guunegai lived down near the bottom of Reservation Road with his father and his mother and a lot of younger sisters and brothers. That family was a mess. Mostly Knud did a lot of drinking. He had cut his father with a knife at least twice when he was young. Knud was quick, and like a junkyard cat, was always slinking around somewhere looking for an advantage, mostly how to get a bottle, but sometimes it was more. Living on the Reservation was pretty much living without. Some people could accept it, some people couldn't. We had the Kowache town to show us what we didn't have. It was hard living on the Reservation knowing what the white people had. It was hard not to want that when every time you went down there something or someone would remind you that you were an Indian, and because you were an Indian you couldn't have those things, even if you wanted them. Knud Guunegai was full of hunger and desire. I really don't think he knew what to do with himself. It seemed like he was going to drink himself to death but he just kept on living. Alcohol couldn't kill him.

It was the Fourth of July, and on the Fourth of July people would set up lawn chairs and sit up at the top of Reservation Road and watch the fireworks in Jackson. Some people on the Reservation just sat out there and ate coleslaw and beans and talked. Other people drank liquor. Knud was one of those. There was always trouble around a holiday; some people just don't know what to do with themselves. Jackie Locklear always found a way to get a couple packs of firecrackers and he and Joe Bad Crow would blow them up in the ditch.

I remember sound was travelling that night, a rain would set in the next morning. Talk was pretty loud. Big Joe Palmer got to yelling, waving a bottle in his hand, like a pistol. He got on to something he was calling National Private Property Day, and tried leading cheers for the uranium they were talking about finding, the way it would bring jobs, but it was hard to tell if he was being serious. I couldn't tell if he was for them finding uranium or against it, because every once in a while he would just yell out, "Fuck them! Terminate uranium!" I don't know what he was talking about but I think he was one of those who was for termination. This was back in the fifties when the government was using its program for Indian relocation; they were trying to get rid of what was left of Indian culture. You don't hear that much about it now but that's what they were doing. There were more than a few on the Reservation who were actually for termination.

The night before there had been a meeting down at the school because I don't think the Legion Hall had been built at that time. Chief Billy had a couple of representatives from the Army Corps of Engineers answer questions about what the government was doing on Reservation land, and how it was vital to national security. Chief Billy wore his Sunday coat and a white cowboy hat, like he was running a bingo game. Whenever those two white guys answered somebody's question Chief Billy followed it up, like he was explaining what those two white guys *really* meant.

These guys were handing out samples of uranium and talking about what it looked like and how we might know what it was when we saw it.

Uranium by itself is white and lustrous, they said. It was the profitable ore they were after, but they wanted to know about anything we found because they said there were economics involved, and that a uranium mineral that is not an ore mineral today might be ten years from now. They wanted to map everything. That's what white people do.

But they were looking for pitchblende and uranite, and they had samples of those. They looked pretty much the same to me, kind of black or dark brown, like black walnut, a kind of purple to it if you squint your eyes, but with a shiny or pitch-like luster too. The other might have looked softer, like soot. And this one fellow, he showed everybody how both of them made a black streak when you rubbed it on a harder rock, and he said that'd be the way to tell it from some other things we might find. By the kind of rock we had, they said we'd have uranium in vein deposits, probably in with the granite that we had.

That night up on the Reservation Road, Big Joe Palmer and some others had gotten to talking about what that meeting had been about, because when everybody left nobody could figure why they'd gone. We were up there at the top of Reservation Road waiting for the fireworks. Big Joe Palmer was carrying on about the Bill of Rights, poverty and suffering, land ownership, and somebody told Big Joe Palmer he was drunk, which might have reminded somebody else to ask, "Where's Knud?"

They said it because Knud Guunegai was chief of the road, chief of the falling-down drunks, chief of the big talkers. He always presided over the Fourth of July. It was Knud's one day when everybody came out and sat on his road, ate hot dogs and pork and beans, drank ice tea or liquor, and Knud would get drunker than anybody. But he wasn't there. Nobody knew where he was. It was just a pause, when the living miss the living, and then the night and the talking and the drinking and the eating went on. Somebody might have said it was strange that Knud Guunegai wasn't there.

Knud Guunegai was one of those Indians who just disappeared, except nobody figured Knud to get himself killed by a goon or a white man who didn't like his politics. He wasn't a political Indian; he was a drunk. After a day or two everybody kind of knew Knud was dead; we just didn't know where his body was.

"He's probably in a ditch somewhere," people said. "Knud probably drank so much he didn't wake up when the water rose in the ditch." This was

because there were big rains after the Fourth of July.
It was an interesting idea and seemed as good as any
until, about a month later, some white man going
fishing found Knud's body down by the river road on
the other side of Jackson. He had pulled off the road
to go dig worms and there was Knud, lying face
down in a drainage ditch about a hundred feet off the
road. The body was taken to the Presbyterian
Hospital in Jackson and they said Knud Guunegai
had died of exposure. That didn't make much sense.
Knud'd be out there on Reservation Road in January
with two feet of snow and it didn't phase him. He
had a constitution like a horse. Besides, Knud, never
in his life, would have walked that far. Some people
said it was a hit-and-run, but if it was that, whoever
hit him went to a lot of trouble to carry his body way
off the road like that. Nobody really tried to figure it
out at the time. A lot of people just figured Knud had
gone off and done something stupid and gotten himself killed. The local police sure weren't going to look
into it and the tribal police didn't, probably because
of that whole mess in the Kachawna Basin. It wasn't
going any further than that. In the end he got hisself
buried in the Presbyterian Church graveyard.

I was down at the Legion Hall when Joseph
Calaitl was there drinking a Coke and eating a pack of
Nabs just like his doctor told him not to and he
announced, "That's the end of the Crow Society.
Knud's the last, ain't nobody else left." I had never
thought about it that way, that Knud Guunegai had

any kind of role in anything, or how there were some old people, and Joseph Calaitl was one of them, who took the stories seriously, how they gave us our identity and told us who we are.

Joseph Calaitl was one fat Indian with diabetes, always down at the Legion Hall watching people play ping-pong or pool, drinking Coke and eating three or four packs of Nabs at a time out of the cracker machine.

"Joseph, you gonna kill yourself drinking Coke and eating those Nabs," somebody might say to him.

"Well, maybe I'll get lucky. I haven't found anything else that will."

I'd never had that much to do with Joseph Calaitl. I didn't grow up with him. He was probably twenty-five years older than me. I'd say "Hey" down at the Legion Hall and at a barbecue or a powwow, but I never really had a conversation with him. He was just a big fat Indian to me.

People talked about Mercy Cleary for how much she remembered, the way she knew things. She knew the stories and she spoke the old words. Mercy Cleary lived way back up behind Old Man's Back and didn't come down, not for food or anything. She never did get electricity or running water, even into the seventies when she finally disappeared, around about the same time Sun Susie disappeared and Joe had that motorcycle accident. They never did find her body. People could disappear up around Old Man's Back, called that because from the south the mountain looks like an old man's back, but it's said that from the air you can see spurs coming off the main backbone, so the whole mountain has the look of the spinal column of an old drying-up man. I had never seen that. Even Grandfather and Ruay Overmoon had never seen that, but they said that in the old days there were medicine men who could fly, and they had seen that. That was rough country, a lot of rock, and ways to get turned around and lost, a lot of steep slopes and cliffs. It was the kind of place you could fall off a mountain, or some said the mountain lions up there would take people, especially children or old people. I'd found deer up there stripped to the bone. But I think Mercy Cleary just decided it was time to leave the material plane. Sun Susie got murdered and Mercy Cleary, in her own way, was just balancing the universe. She told me as much before she left.

Mercy Cleary didn't look old because she had most of her teeth, but the more I looked at her the older Mercy Cleary got, with skin like the Earth with rivers in it. But she didn't know what she looked like; she didn't believe in mirrors, didn't have one. She sat in a rocker, and any time she was talking to me she would try to get my eye, but I could never look at her very long. Her wisdom was too strong. Some old people have power: not all, not many, but maybe those who are close to death and aren't afraid of it. Mercy Cleary was that way, Aunt Ida too, Grandmother and Grandfather, Joseph Calaitl.

Mercy Cleary had children but most of them moved away or died. Edna Ryden was one of her daughters; she sold baskets in town until she moved away. And there were a couple of Mercy Cleary's grandsons who were in the movies, Indians in those Glenn Ford Westerns, who made good money because they knew how to fall off a horse.

Some traditionals thought Mercy Cleary was what is called a ghostwalker, a kind of shapeshifter. To most people shapeshifting is a superstitious belief, but in the dances, when a dancer is wearing the feathers, or the skins, of an animal guardian, they take on the power of the animal: the eagle, the wolf, the bear, whichever one they have become. There's a lot of misconception about that, just the same way you can hear about ghosts as something evil, but it's people's own minds that create that, and so they gossip and tell about shapeshifters doing all sorts of terrible things: making people sick, committing murders, robbing graves, eating the dead, all sorts of shit you wouldn't believe. It's not like that.

There were stories though, and you could hear good ones and you could hear bad ones. Ruay Overmoon had a story he liked to tell sometimes about Chief Billy's nephew, Pearson Robbins. Pearson Robbins and his wife were staying at Chief Billy's house while Chief Billy and Alma Farmer were off on a vacation to Las Vegas because Alma liked doing that. One day Chief Billy's dogs were putting up a fuss, and when Pearson's wife looked out, she saw what looked like a mountain lion among those dogs. As she watched, the animal ran around the house and disappeared behind a shed, and Pearson grabbed a rifle and went out to look. He swore he saw mountain lion tracks clear as day, but when the tracks reached the other side of the shed, they turned into moccasin tracks. He said the person had small feet, like those of a woman. The tracks led right to hard ground and a boulder field and disappeared, heading north. But what I wondered was why a mountain lion was hanging around Chief Billy's house.

People could misbelieve anything they wanted about shapeshifting, but I mainly knew Mercy Cleary as a teller of stories. It's mostly forgotten now, but the storyteller of a people is the most powerful person in the tribe. Mercy Cleary was the last storyteller of the Mountain Lion Clan. She told me some of those Mountain Lion Clan stories because she was concerned those stories would be lost forever.

It was a sad thing, but Mercy Cleary believed that, except for Joseph Calaitl, and she wasn't sure about him because she hadn't spoken to him in twenty years, she was the last true speaker of the Uwharrie language. After Ruay Overmoon died, Grandfather, Aunt Ida, and Mercy Cleary said there weren't any left who knew the words. She said Thomas Matoas Paint didn't know all the words, and for her that meant that Uwharrie tradition would die with her, that there would be no true Uwharrie people after her. The language carries the tradition. Without our native language there is no Uwharrie. This is what she told me.

Even the stories she told me I don't fully understand. I know the words but the old words can sound like mumbling to young ears. Many of the stories she told me were origin stories. She would begin with, "Long ago when the animals were people..." because in so many of the stories the animals, like the raccoon and the coyote, were acting like people. In ourselves are all the animals. These animals had pipes and bows and arrows and things like that, and talked about things people talk about. Mercy Cleary would point off to a part of the sky, to Sky Coyote, and tell his part in the making of a man.

"He should have hands like me," Sky Coyote said.

Sky Coyote always tried to talk first, and he always tried to talk last, so he could have his way in everything. We would have paws, like Coyote, if Lizard hadn't been hiding and heard what Coyote said. Lizard knew we weren't meant to have paws like a coyote, and so he jumped out and put his hand impressions in the rocks. You can see that in the sky, and that's what Mercy Cleary showed me, in the spring and summer, near Scorpion Woman. He's not so easy to see, because he's hiding in the rocks, but he's there.

So many stories are gone now, but something in me was becoming. I began to collect the stories of our ancestors like seeds in a bag, and one of my names, the Seed, began to grow meaning in me. The cycles of the sun and of the moon came and went and came again, and I felt like the mother and the child and the grandmother, all at the same time, because the seed holds death and birth. Some of the stories are lost forever, because we have clans and some of the storytellers died without leaving anyone the stories: the Deer Clan, the Lizard Clan, the Crow Clan. But I know the Owl Clan stories, and the Wren Clan stories, because I am of those clans, and Mercy Cleary told me stories, and Joseph Calaitl of the Grouse Clan told me about Scorpion Woman, Spitting Hole, Chief of the Land of the Dead, Land of the Widows, and Mars the Condor, who has a long nose, a blanket, and two sticks like walking sticks, so he can travel long distances. He can carry messages across. These help us to know who our ancestors are and what they did in the purpose of things. Our stories tell us we come from the River in the Sky, the path of souls. This river moves through what is now called time, but is the silence of the stars of the night, the silence deeper than anything.

Stories can fill a person with faith, and by listening over and over again, I began to know what Mercy Cleary was saying. I could tell by a change in cadence, in a rhythm, what she was talking about or when she'd gone on to something else. Or sometimes I'd just sit there on the step, looking out across the gulch, nodding my head, agreeing with whatever she was saying until she got to a part I could recognize. I began to know when a part of a story I knew was coming, and I could begin to piece together other parts which came before that story or after it.

"The old people knew the Kowache were coming long before they came," Mercy Cleary said. "They knew, even before the Kowache got here, how the Kowache thought about the land, how they would use the land, and how, one day, the Kowache ways will disappear. The prophecies do not say the white people disappear, only their ways."

I had never heard this.

"Is this true?"

"The old ones could see farther than most are willing to look," Mercy Cleary said. "You will know if it's true when it's time."

Ruay Overmoon, Grandfather and Gary Yellow Knife all talked about balancing the universe, but they all had different words for it. Ruay Overmoon would tell one story and Grandfather would tell another. That could go on for hours. Ruay Overmoon didn't move things around in his house, like move a toaster or move a chair out in the backyard for junk, but he knew what Grandfather was doing when he did that. It made sense to him. Mostly what he did was "make words in the air."

When Ruay Overmoon and Grandfather were balancing the universe together, it was like they were disagreeing without talking, but it would come out alright. Grandfather liked to use tolache cakes. He kept a tin of those cakes in his satchel. They didn't go bad; they were hard like a burnt cookie, made of tolache and clay. The cake had the effect of keeping a person's mind from spinning the world the way they think it is, or spinning it in a way they hadn't imagined, but was true.

Grandfather would pull out his bag of stones, petrified wood he'd gotten from somewhere on the Kai-neye Range. The elementals, he called them. He had names for them, stones he called the sun, the moon, the rain, the stars. Some of them looked like what they were: a whitish stone he always put in the east, and looked like an eagle's wing, he called the eagle; and a stone he put in the west was dark, like the form of a crouching bear. And then there was mountain lion, a sienna stone he kept wrapped separate from the rest in a piece of tawed leather, I think because it was a softer stone and could crumble.

Mostly my grandfather laid out the stones. It made a comical sight, Ruay Overmoon being so tall and skinny and Grandfather so short with his head round like a coconut. Ruay Overmoon would say the words. They were *almost* words anyway, because everything Ruay Overmoon said when he and Grandfather were doing this thing over the stones he said real slow, not like he was thinking, but like the words were trying to come up into the light of day from way down deep somewhere, like the Earth. That's why Ruay Overmoon called them wind words, because the way he thought about it, the words travelled up from the hidden places into the plain day of sky.

"Wind words fly with the birds of the air; none can follow them except those who can remember," he said. It was from Ruay Overmoon that I learned the sacred word for wind, which is *rooach* meaning "that which thinks in us." Ruay Overmoon said there is a wind within each of us, and that when we are silent the wind is speaking. The wind is life itself, every plant, animal, insect and bird having been given the means of movement and speech by the wind. We think of the wind as an unseen organizing principle, every self at once.

Ruay Overmoon muttered the unformed words, and when he and Grandfather were working over the stones they reminded me of an old man and an old woman, like an old married couple, Ruay Overmoon moving slow and Grandfather moving kind of quick,

quick for an old man anyway.

Grandfather never put out the circle the same way twice. "You can have *too much* order," he'd say. "When you have that something really crazy happens to change it."

Putting out those stones was kind of like placing the stars in the sky. Ruay Overmoon called what they did sacred gambling, not like is done in casinos, but his and Grandfather's part in balancing the universe. Gambling is a game of intuition, something cultivated and gathered, and not something other people can do for you. The universe is basically benevolent; if it wasn't that way, there wouldn't be life and we wouldn't get what we need. But there is unpredictability in all this too. And so Grandfather and Ruay Overmoon played their stone game, but it had the aspect of a play, a drama, the way Ruay Overmoon's long, thin body swayed as he sing-song spoke and Grandfather rocked in place, almost like an old woman rocking by the hearth.

The gaming stones would tumble in the dust. I would watch for who was winning but I could never figure it out.

There is in the Uwharrie language a word which means "the world's thought," but because we are human we don't know what that means really. We just watch the world, listen to what the rocks, the trees, the coyotes and the fox have to tell us. The Crow Society says the word came in through them, but the Owl Society says the same thing. Each society claims the origin of the word. We don't really know and it doesn't matter; they are just different versions of the same story.

When Mercy Cleary disappeared, about the time she disappeared anyway, I went up behind Old Man's Back, up in the scrub pines and along a ridge where a man gets smaller and the wind talks off the oldness of the world. There was a spot there that spoke to me, and I laid stones out in a circle, trying to do in the same spirit Grandfather would have done, trying to speak the wind words, like Ruay Overmoon. And I asked the stones to remind me why I am here.

But when I went up there on that ridge, those were troubled times, and I was wishing to reestablish well-being in the world. I tried to do what I had heard Ruay Overmoon do, to enter into the state of story, by singing the wind words, which for us is like flying in the wind. One person, on behalf of the community, can ask for this. It is a belief we have in restoration or reoccurrence. The Uwharrie have always believed that if something happens once it will happen again, and so restoration is possible. We can impart a state of well-being to the cosmos by story and song.

I have no way of knowing how long I had been there, when time just stopped.

I didn't see her until she was leaving, the great old mountain lion looking back at me from a boulder. She was tawny like dust, sway-backed, her belly slung low. She was as big as a man, like a man in the mountain lion shape. I don't know how long she'd been there, fixing me in her green eyes.

It took such effort for her to begin to move, as if she were tired, weary in the long knowledge of hiding from men. Perhaps she had been waiting for me, holding her large, ragged head from her hunched shoulders. Her tail teetered in space as if she didn't want to go. But she looked right at me before she heaved herself across to another rock. With a backward glance she jumped again. Then she was stretching her long body up the mountain by way of boulders, effortlessly following an invisible trail familiar to her, her grey, tawny body seeming to draw power from the rocks.

I don't know if the mountain lion topped the rise or whether she merged into the mountain itself, became part of the hard pink-grey rock of the mountain. I strained my eyes but I couldn't see her anymore.

I sat in the searing sounds of grasshoppers and the heat, what seemed random and undetermined, for a long time afterwards.

It was Joe Bad Crow who told me about the medical records work at the hospital, what maybe got Sun Susie killed. It didn't come out all at once because Joe worked out so much stuff in his own head, and sometimes wouldn't tell anybody anything. There weren't any words about him and Sun Susie between us, but he could read me, and I suppose he just kind've guessed I knew, because when he started talking it was already understood.

We were down by the river, not fishing or anything; we were just down there. I couldn't say Joe liked going down there; it was more like he had to, after that motorcycle accident and all, how a dream could seem a curse.

"I know you and Ruby are trying to figure out about Sun Susie," Joe said, but he talked tight-jawed, like he had a hard time even saying Ruby's name. "That's good."

I looked over at him to see if he meant it. He did, but I didn't know where he was going with it, because he just kind of brought it up while we were watching a couple of orange peels and a plastic milk jug floating by.

"Yeah."

"I knew she was nervous about that work at the hospital," Joe said. "She talked crazy. I just couldn't figure it out. She was smoking like a chimney, four or five packs a day."

Joe kind've left me to figure out he was talking about Sun Susie.

"What do you mean she was nervous about her work at the hospital?"

"It was tearing her up. She talked about Margaret Brown, saying crazy stuff like how they put Margaret Brown away."

"Margaret Brown? You mean Margaret Brown who died of diabetes? What do you mean put away?"

"Yeah. I tell you she was talking crazy, when she talked, and that wasn't much. She wasn't sleeping either. I couldn't stay there."

Joe Bad Crow still hadn't said right out that he had been sleeping with Sun Susie, and I thought about all that silence between him and Ruby, and all I could ever figure was that I never knew what was going on between them when they hadn't been talking.

"Sun Susie was working on some kind of virus study, pulling records, and somehow she found out some kind of shit that had her thinking that Margaret Brown hadn't just up and died of diabetes."

"What'd she say?"

"I don't know. Like I said, I couldn't stay around her. We fought some."

It was strange. It was like I couldn't tell exactly what Joe was saying when he was saying this. Here he was talking about Sun Susie, but it sounded like he could have been talking about Ruby.

Ruby was working three jobs then and Joe Bad

Crow just continued to be pissed off at a white man he was never going to see. I didn't have a job then. I'd quit my job picking up cigarette butts down at the municipal building in Jackson one day when a white woman came by and threw a cigarette butt down in my face.

"Joe thinks there's a reason Margaret Brown's name is on that little piece of paper we found in the crossword book that day in Sun Susie's house," I said to Ruby.

"Joe does?" The look she gave me was the look she meant for Joe. It was as close as she could get to him, like without words she was saying, "Tell Joe he's a son of a bitch."

"Yeah, well, I'm not sure," I said, "but I think he thinks that Sun Susie didn't think that Margaret Brown died of diabetes, and that's why her name is on a little piece of paper, that she probably wrote down more than that, because she was pulling records on some kind of virus study and found something out. Maybe."

"Well, that's a big maybe," Ruby said, disgusted. It was hard for her to think of Joe being any kind of way useful. "It's not going to make much difference now that the house burnt down."

I watched Ruby's face while she let the fact of what Joe had said have some other meaning than six bad years of marriage.

"What about Ruth Upchurch?" I said. "Would she know anything about what Sun Susie was involved with at the hospital?"

"Probably, but *I* know what Sun Susie was working on at the hospital. She was working on an enterovirus study, something to do with drinking water. Nothing to do with diabetes."

Ruby was in a slow burn. She couldn't see what she was fighting against; if it had a name it didn't have a face, not a man with a conscience, not a who but a what: a corporation, a mentality, a system of thought, patriarchy—ending in assimilation, an endless feeling of not being worthy, never quite tangible.

Ruth Upchurch was living in a trailer just down the road from her grandfather. Ruby and me and Thomas Matoas Paint went over there. Ruth Upchurch's trailer had a makeshift tin roof held up with aluminum poles so you could sit outside if it was raining, had a grill out there and a couple of fold-up chairs. She gave us some good ice tea and we sat out of the sun and she told us about what an enterovirus was, since that's what Sun Susie had been pulling records on.

"An enterovirus is a virus that lives in the gut," Ruth Upchurch said. "Turns out an enterovirus can stay alive for weeks in a sheep or a goat, and part of this study was looking into water supplies on Indian reservations, how different tribes get their water. They were doing research out of the University of Chicago about diabetes, and looking if there was a connection between diabetes in Indian tribes who've got goats and sheep. There was something about water-borne pathogens, and they were doing autopsies, taking samples from the pancreas, and from the heart too. They were looking at the virus called the Coxsackie virus because they already figured it had something to do with heart disease. Some of these viruses spread by feces in the drinking water, the feces of sheep and goats."

"Diabetes, huh?" Thomas said. "Do you remember Margaret Brown, lived over in the Kachawna Basin? She died of diabetes. She had a son who died of diabetes too. He fell off his horse and nobody could get to him in time. But it's more than a little strange that Sun Susie would have their names writ down on a little piece of paper in her house, along with Knud Guunegai."

"Knud Guunegai?"

"You know, Ruth. He was the drunk who used to stand out on the Reservation Road and flap his arms like a crow and make everybody else's business his own," Thomas said.

"Oh yeah, he was crazy. Well, I don't know about Knud Guunegai," Ruth said. "The hospital in Chicago was asking for autopsies to be done on Indians who died with diabetes as a contributing condition, taking tissue from their heart and pancreas and testing them for enteroviruses and echoviruses. They did blood tests too. It was all over—Navahos, Lakotas, people up in Spokane, Washington—and Sun Susie was pulling the records on any Indian who died with diabetes before the study began, and looking for something. I can't remember what it was, but she was making copies of records and sending them to Chicago."

"Do you think she found something out?" Ruby asked her.

"What do you mean?" Ruth asked her.

"Could Margaret Brown have been listed as having died of diabetes but have actually died of something else?"

"I'm not sure what you mean, but, oh yeah, there could have been some kind of mix-up. You know the crazy shit that happens in hospitals, Ruby. Just a couple of weeks ago, O. T. Beldon came in for some tests, and the next thing you know he's dead."

"O. T. Beldon? Who's O. T. Beldon?" I said.

"He's that seedy white man who worked down at the Poison Creek Store."

"Oh yeah."

"O. T. Beldon had an irregular heart rhythm and he probably just got too much of something. Maybe it wasn't deliberate but it was probably an injection of potassium chloride, because Lulu Freeman and O. T.'s doctor were the only ones that had access to his quinidine."

"They would do that?" I said.

"Not everybody who works in a hospital is a saint, Warren," Ruth Upchurch said. "Sun Susie told me about some of the stuff that went on in medical records, like maybe they need some figures to bring the totals down so they won't have to pay some Navahos compensation for lung disease, so they do some kind of cancer study for uranium mines and they throw in our numbers. It's a matter of record there was uranium exploration here. How many miners died of lung complications? Not many, not many compared to how many've drunk themselves to death, liver failure or something, or died in a car crash. But that way they can say, 'Look, there's no obvious correlation between lung disease and uranium mining.' They do that shit all the time so Indians won't get any health care. They cook the numbers all the time."

"Was Sun Susie involved in that uranium study you're talking about?" Ruby asked. "The one with the Navahos and the lung disease?"

"No, I don't think so. I think she just knew about it because she was working in epidemiology and that was just part of the stuff she told me about."

"But what about Margaret Brown?" Thomas said.

"Maybe Margaret Brown got too much insulin. That could've happened. It doesn't take much to kill somebody in a hospital, but I don't think you're going to be able to find out how some diabetic died twenty some years ago. We couldn't find that out if it happened yesterday."

"I don't remember that Margaret Brown died in a hospital," Thomas said. "I think they found her on the floor in her home."

"If she got too much insulin, she would have had to have died in the hospital," Ruth said.

"Do you know if Dr. Stevenson has anything to

do with this study?" I asked Ruth Upchurch.

"Dr. Stevenson? I don't think so. Maybe, but I don't think so. He's not a GI specialist."

Me and Thomas Matoas Paint went with Ruby when she went to the coroner's office, and Thomas seemed pretty fired up because he thought there was something to those death certificates for Margaret Brown, Sam Brown and Knud Guunegai.

"If we're lucky they did autopsies," I said.

"They probably didn't," Ruby said. But we wanted to see whatever records they had, even if it was just a death certificate. They at least had to have a death certificate.

The clerk at the coroner's office was pissed off we were there. She didn't like it that Injuns were asking about a death by exposure fifteen years before. It seemed like she married young and blamed her husband for fucking up her life. She had us sit down in some slimy uncomfortable chairs that'd absorbed some bad energy, and we waited for half an hour while she talked on the phone to her sister. Then she disappeared like she'd gone to look for something, but it was just a long smoke break, because she came back and talked on the phone some more. Finally Thomas got up and stuck one of his big arms up on the aluminum sill of the divider window and said, "We still want to see those death certificates." That old pasty white woman went back and got the slim folders they had on Knud Guunegai, Margaret Brown and Sam Brown.

"You can't leave out of here with those," she said, like she was daring us or something.

I guess Thomas knew Ruby was about to say something stupid and make matters worse, so he grabbed her wrist with his big hand. "Thank you," he said, as overly polite as he could, flashed that wicked grin of his he thinks every lady likes, and took the folders himself.

"She mostly works because she doesn't want to go home," he said as we sat back down in those Naugahyde chairs.

There wasn't much on Margaret Brown or Sam Brown, only death certificates. There hadn't been an autopsy on either of them. It was pretty much as I remembered it. Margaret Brown had died of diabetes, but there had been some kind of complications, what they called cardiac arrythmia, what they had determined at the Presbyterian Hospital when they brought her in. A coroner had signed Sam Brown's death certificate saying that he had died of diabetes too, diabetic ketoacidosis. On both the death certificates it said that what had happened had been due to diabetes, but the attending physician for Margaret Brown, and the one who signed her death certificate, was Dr. Stevenson.

Words on a paper might not mean much, and I couldn't even say what I was suspicious of. It was just a feeling, nothing with words to it at all, but it was like I knew his name was going to be there, right there on that death certificate.

"Margaret Brown didn't die in the hospital," Thomas said.

"Well, Ruth said she did, and the way they've got it written up, it sure sounds like she did."

"Well she didn't; she died on her kitchen floor. I've thought about that. Maybe they just took her to the hospital afterwards—but they didn't need to because she was dead on the kitchen floor."

"That's the way I remember it too," I said.

There was an autopsy report on Knud Guunegai, and a black-and-white photograph of Knud Guunegai, the way they found him. It was creepy. I remembered Knud Guunegai as a real asshole, but he was a live asshole. The photograph, it was almost like it wasn't him. I had never seen a dead man in a photograph. I had heard that some native people won't let themselves get their picture taken because they're afraid the camera will capture their spirit, but everybody looks dead in a photograph. The camera can't capture anything, much less a spirit. But there he was, Knud Guunegai, dead in a photograph. He had always just been dead in my mind.

It wasn't much of an autopsy report; there were only two pieces of paper. My sister looked through both of them, and then looked at the photograph. She never knew Knud Guunegai. The report said he'd been hit in the head; there was a contusion. But the coroner had listed the immediate cause of death as liver failure, and exposure as a related cause. Knud had a liver disease.

"That ain't right," Thomas said. "It says here he died of liver failure. It was exposure."

"It was exposure. It says that down here," and I pointed to where it called exposure a contributing condition.

"No, not a contributing condition. He died of exposure," Thomas said. "It says right there he got hit in the head. Somebody hit him over the head, dragged him off and he died of exposure. They want to be technical about it, they could say somebody hitting him over the head with a crowbar was a contributing condition."

"If he'd gotten his head bashed in they would have said that," I said.

"He could have hit his own head," Ruby said. "Technically he died of liver failure, Thomas. Knud's liver was shot. His liver failed when he got cold."

"Well, that's convenient. That could have happened any time on the Reservation Road, but what's he doing keeling over dead five miles away? He sure didn't walk."

Whenever something happened which couldn't be directly explained, Ruay Overmoon would tell the story about his mother's sister, Sissy Nanibush, who was always sitting out in the sun in an old abandoned two-door Chevy by the highway. She was always out there, sitting in the front seat with both doors open, whenever Aunt Ida, Grandmother and me drove into town, or whether we didn't, and she was still out there forty years later. The Poison Creek Store is gone and there's a little shopping center there now where you can buy genuine Indian baskets and fireworks.

She always wore an old nightie with a faded bluish-green bathrobe over it, had grey stringy hair like a mop and hollowed sunken eyes. The weather didn't matter to her, because her grief was too great. Story was she had married a white man with a twisted mind. Whenever we drove by she was always looking past us, up the road, wringing her hands, as if something was horribly wrong, and the next car, not one she could ever see, was bringing her solace. I waved out the back sometimes, but then one day I just stopped waving.

"Sissy Nanibush was married at one time, then her husband died," Ruay Overmoon said. "He had a spiritual sickness common to a white man. He had locked her up in a room, put a chain and a bolt on the door. But she couldn't bear that, so Sissy Nanibush climbed out through the window and jumped off the roof. Nearly killed herself, and that's probably what she was trying to do."

"Was she crazy?" I asked him.

"Ain't nobody crazy, because there's an origin in everything," Ruay Overmoon said. "But Sissy Nanibush talked all the time about angels."

Ruay Overmoon had it that maybe in Sissy Nanibush's mind she thought of herself as one of those fallen angels we heard about in church, the ones Reverend Blake talked about sometimes.

He said that Sissy Nanibush loved to sing and used to sing on Sundays for the Presbyterian Church in Presbyterian Wells, when there was a church there, before that town dried up and died. She learned to play the autoharp, and the sound of her singing and playing was as beautiful as anything Ruay Overmoon had ever heard, said he could close his eyes and see clouds in moonlight, or wildflowers in spring when the creeks run chill with the winter's waters. Sissy Nanibush sang the old songs and sang hymns and stuff when the women were shelling beans, or making baskets, or whatever they were doing.

"Maybe she wasn't in her right mind, Warren, but she wasn't crazy," Ruay said. "Maybe she thought she had wings like an angel, but she wasn't crazy. After Sissy Nanibush jumped off that roof the women took her broken body and tried to help her, but her husband found out where she was and came and got her. Took her back. He locked her up in a room again and nailed up the windows so she couldn't get out, and paid someone to take her food and water. Sissy Nanibush never did heal properly, just took on the pain inside that sick man of a husband. That's been more than thirty years ago. You can hear all sorts of stories about how Sissy Nanibush tried to kill her husband with a knife, or how she lost a lover in World War I, but those are just stories white people make up so they can feel better."

Maybe Sissy Nanibush was just waiting for her angel. Maybe one day her angel was going to come down the road in a Pontiac and nobody but her would know. I hoped so anyway, but it seemed like it was taking a long time for her angel to come. But that's a story that somebody would tell when there was something that happened that couldn't be directly understood. People have reasons to be the way they are, and things happen out of those reasons, even when we don't know them. There was a lot not said on the Reservation, but it didn't mean you didn't know it.

It was Ruay Overmoon who told me that Grandmother had been set against Ruby's getting adopted, that it had been Grandfather's idea. Whenever mention of Ruby's adopted family came up, Grandmother got that rock hard look and long jaw, like nobody knew her and she didn't know anybody else. Grandfather never crossed Grandmother on much, but I think he crossed her on that. Ruay said that adoption was Grandfather's way of trying to understand white people; it was all there in the stones. It was like how I was learning and keeping the stories of our people, Ruby was learning the other side of that, the way of the Kowache.

Ruay Overmoon was one big story. When he died, a story was what was left of him. He liked to say, "Our prayers take away our enemies; our wishes make them." Ruay Overmoon told stories and spoke wind words. I learned some of the words that I know from him, some of the wind words. He was of the Lizard Clan.

Ruay Overmoon could go on for hours telling stories. He was good for that, but you didn't want to run into him walking down the road because he'd keep you and wouldn't let you go. He talked like he was fishing, and once you were hooked you couldn't get away. He'd pretend to be interested in what you were doing, but after a little while, he was doing all the talking and you were just nodding your head, trying to figure out how to get away from there. But my grandfather and Ruay Overmoon were old friends and Grandfather knew how to get Ruay Overmoon to shut up without hurting his feelings.

Ruay Overmoon would get serious when he told about Grey Legs, and the Ghost Riders, as Ruay Overmoon called them, those who had no names. When I was a kid I didn't fully appreciate how careful he got when he told those stories, but I came to, how he told them slower and how he made sure with his eyes I was listening. He wanted me to get those stories right.

"My grandfather knew Grey Legs," Ruay Overmoon would say. "He rode with him. I know the spot where the Kowache say Grey Legs was killed, but he didn't get killed. He got shot, but he didn't get killed."

The Battle of Three Fingers happened in the foothills of the Hipatsu Range, land which had been sold to the Kowache years before in the hopes that this would satisfy them. There was a big thing about it not being possible for a Kowache bullet to harm Grey Legs. He had ridden into many battles and never gotten a scratch. Every soldier's pistol and rifle could be aimed at him, but no bullet could touch him. That was why the white people made such a big thing of how they killed him. But the way we tell that story, the bullet that hit Grey Legs didn't kill him. Grey Legs went away, went up into the hills. He healed but didn't come back down to fight again. Grey Legs took that bullet that had wounded him to mean that the Powers didn't want him to fight the Kowache anymore, that the Uwharrie people had to accept what was happening to us and to our land. That it was all happening for a reason.

"When Grey Legs was a chief, the Kowache didn't know what to do with him," Ruay Overmoon said. "They found Hani Walpo and said. 'You're a chief, aren't you? We want some land.' The Kowache were just looking for some Indian to say 'yes.' I know Hani Walpo was trying to do the right thing, but if he had, the Kowache might never have gotten a toehold here, and we wouldn't have government jeeps and an oil company on our land today."

Thomas Matoas Paint had a different way of saying the same story. Thomas said the night before the Battle of Three Fingers, Grey Legs was leading a small group of warriors up through a field, leading them to where he wanted them when the battle began. He could see, before a battle, where warriors needed to be. He was doing that with bands of warriors, tirelessly going by foot and putting them in the exact spot where they would defeat the spirits of the Kowache soldiers. As Grey Legs was doing this, and ducking under a white man's fence, he scratched his leg on a nail. It was nothing. It was just a scratch, but the nail was rusty.

Grey Legs fought at the Battle of Three Fingers, and somehow we lost that battle. A couple of weeks after Three Fingers, Grey Legs got sick because of that scratch from that rusty nail. He was treated traditionally; a decoction was made from boiling a little pine tree with the bark from a cherry tree and a plum tree. Three trees. Thomas said that none of that would have come into contact with rust or dirt. Grey Legs died anyway, from lockjaw, and Thomas said that there was a kind of tribal shame over Grey Legs dying from lockjaw, because back then, there was a lot of disagreement about the use of metal. Kowache brought it, dug it out of the Earth, and sold it at a high price. Some even said we should give all the metal back, all the pots and pans and spoons and knives and everything, even the rifles, because they had brought nothing but sorrow and trouble and were ruining our lives. Grey Legs himself said we had become weak willed and easy to defeat.

That's how Thomas Matoas Paint told the story, but either way, everybody took it as a sign, and with Grey Legs' death there was no way to defeat the white man, and much of the sacred lands of the Kachawna Basin passed into the hands of the Kowache. They got their gold mines, which is why they had wanted that land all along. Of course the gold mines didn't pay and they gave us the land back.

Ruay Overmoon fought in World War I and had a lot of stories about when he was in France. You never could quite know when one of his war stories was coming on, because something you couldn't see might remind him of something that happened in France. It might be a fence post, or a dog running across the road, or the angle of the sun when it hit a bottle, and he'd get this look in his eye. If you had anything you had to do, you knew you'd better get away from there fast.

I'd wondered how it was Ruay Overmoon got into the army, whether he got drafted or something.

"No," he said, "there were lots of Indians in the war. I wasn't the only one. Not only Uwharrie, there was all kinds of Indians in there."

He told the story of how he nearly didn't get out of a trench in time because he saw some weird eight-foot snake stick his head up out of a stump just when the mustard gas came pouring in. He said him and that snake were frozen in time. A white man had to yank him out of there by the arm.

And one night they were supposed to take some kind of hill in France and hold it against the Germans. Only thing was everybody knew that hill was going to get blasted by German cannons and that most of them would die if they took that hill. The spirits were watching over him, Ruay said. He had a white platoon captain. If he had had an Indian platoon captain they'd have gone up that hill. That white platoon captain, he said, "Nah, we're not going up that hill. We'd get ourselves killed if we went up that hill."

After the couple of hours it would've taken to climb the hill, the white captain sent word back by runner to the general or whoever, saying his company had taken that hill—but they were still down at the bottom of the hill. Sure enough, the Germans began to bomb the hell out of that hill. Ruay figured that white captain saved all their lives—not the kind of hero you see in the movies, but he saved all their lives.

Ruay Overmoon didn't cast a dark eye on the white man the way some people do, or on anybody really. Ruay Overmoon was gentle where a lot of other people have a mean streak. He was the tallest, skinniest Indian I ever saw, looked like a buzzard close up. He never did work in the mines. He got a pension and he sold stuff, and cut cordwood.

Ruay Overmoon lived in a trailer. You didn't want to go in there. If there was ever a man who wanted or needed a woman more than Ruay Overmoon, I don't know them. He talked about women a lot, and I was a lot younger than he was, but that trailer sure needed a woman. It pretty much looked like any other trailer from the outside, except he had sawed-off railroad ties for steps to get up into it, and on the inside it pretty much looked like the FBI had gone through it. I mean there were boxes of magazines in the kitchen, jars of pickled mushrooms, pots and pans and plates on his bed, newspapers all over the floor, not a chair in the place, and it smelled of old rotten food.

"It's a good thing you don't have any children," Grandfather used to say to Ruay Overmoon. "They'd take them away from you for sure."

Ruay Overmoon sure loved women though. He might disappear for a week, like a boy dog going after a girl dog in heat, and you could only guess where he was. It didn't happen often but it happened. Ruay Overmoon wasn't what anyone would call handsome, and he was too old for all those women he was looking at. One eye was lower than the other, and he *did* look like a buzzard.

The only time he might not notice a good-looking woman was when he was telling one of his stories. When he was telling one of his stories he would get that way-off look in his eye, off in his own world, but he could get you to see that world he was in, like it was inside of you. His eyes looked different; they had a kind of clouded-over look, like an old dog with cataracts, but he could see some part of his life over again most any time he wanted, or the ancestors as they saw things, and he was telling you about it same as it could have been you. He told a good story. He was real serious then. But Ruay Overmoon enjoyed teasing people too, making games with anyone who would listen or play along. He would tease me. Some of our people lived in villages along the Mahonawassi and the Pebbawassi Rivers. Ruay Overmoon made fun of me for calling them by these names, but that's what I learned to call them in the Reservation School so I wouldn't have to write extra.

"Are you going to catch some fish on the Fish River River?" he would say.

Pebbawassi means fish river.

"If you were in the Reservation School you wouldn't do very good, old man," I'd say.

"They have nothing to teach me," he always said, like it was a good thing. I didn't know what it was but there was stubbornness about some of the elders that few others on the Reservation had. Grandmother was like that, Grandfather, Ruay Overmoon, Mercy Cleary, Billy Arch who lived off by himself below Ruby, the red mountain. When there started to be talk about termination it wasn't the old people who were for it; it was my father's generation. A lot of my father's generation wanted the money they could make by selling the land. They wanted things, things like the Kowache had. Some people had bought cars and they wanted the roads, but neither the state or the BIA was going to look into that if we were still one people. I came to know that my father was a warrior, born into a time he didn't understand, confusing times, when so much is smoke and deception, *mot´e*. I came to know this because the moment I am in, right here, right now, is the story of everything—how we came here, and who we are.

I think Ruay Overmoon knew that when he died the only thing left of him would be some words he'd said into the air. He knew his trailer was going to fall down and rot. He knew his body would crumble into dust. He had never had any children and so he would leave no physical record of himself. All that would be left of him would be the words he had said. What he wanted when he was living was somebody who would listen to him. He hoped it would be a woman. Mostly he hoped it would be a pretty woman. But if that didn't happen, he just wanted someone to listen to what he was saying. Mostly it was Grandfather and some men in the tribe—Guthern Young Bear, Lester Keestrong and some others.

As far as I know he never told anybody the Lizard Clan stories.

Grandfather had his own hold on reality; it wasn't like anybody else's. Grandfather spoke of an invisible universe, where the whites never get across the river and maybe Grey Legs isn't killed at Three Fingers. The battle is won and there are no oil trucks on the Reservation. Hell, there isn't any reservation, and the heart and soul, in some unimaginable instant, are released from the bondage of the past. I know some of the old language in words that Grandfather told to me, but some of them died with him.

One day we were hauling rocks out of the field with a wheelbarrow. I would push the wheelbarrow and he would talk. That's the way we worked. Then he would help me load up the wheelbarrow again. I would put on ten rocks and he would put on one or two. Anyway, I thought he was going to say something, like he usually did, but when I turned and looked at him, Grandfather was just standing there, as if he were waiting for something.

"What is it, Grandfather?"

He could see something. I could tell. I knew the old ones could see something in the air, feel it when it came up on the wind or fell with the leaves.

"I thought the war was over," Grandfather said, "but it isn't. The white people aren't fighting Indians anymore. Their war is with the Earth."

Young people think old people are crazy. But the closer to dying we get the more we see of the spirit world. Maybe for awhile we think they're just ignoring us or are off somewhere doing whatever spirits do when they aren't helping us, but they're with us all the time. Most of us just don't know it. Early in the morning, before the day has begun, and at twilight, when the blanket of the night is bringing a close to the waking world, are good times to feel the presence of these spirits. They're always there, but when the sun is overhead, our thoughts are turned to other things, worldly things, like what we think we are supposed to do: split wood, pile rocks, whatever.

One day, not long before he died, Grandfather told me a story. I'd heard the story before, but this time while he was telling it he kept doing that thing he did with his eyes, trapping my attention. Most people, when they look at you, look at you with one eye or the other, and they don't even know they're doing it. They aren't giving you their full attention; they don't know how to, white people in particular. But Grandfather had a way of looking at you with both eyes at once, like a hunter, like a hunter of the heart.

I knew this story was important to him, or he felt it was important for me to know it anyway. This is the way stories are for us; how we are the Uwharries. He was intent on me seeing the story in my own mind, so I could tell it again. It was his story about an archeologist going up behind Old Man's Back to dig up a dinosaur jawbone. I knew about how we kept our eyes out when white people showed up asking questions, archeologists or whoever. The Reservation, whatever else it was, was home, and white men are outsiders, and they come because they want things. In the fifties it would be uranium; in the sixties and seventies it would be oil; and in the nineties, it would be Indian spirituality. If archeologists showed up looking for dinosaur bones, I had heard how Sammy and David Greys, Joseph Calaitl and Grandfather would stand the road and send them back if it seemed like they were going up around Old Man's Back, and at one time, the *Urapitan*, or the House.

"One day Chief Billy gave permission for some archeologist to go looking for stuff up on the other side of Old Man's Back. I don't know what Chief Billy was thinking," Grandfather said. "Nobody needs a white man disappearing up around Old Man's Back. The archeologist had a jeep, but I found his jeep parked on that old logging road heading north— you know, that old logging road where Chief Billy's father let them do logging up that way back in the forties. It goes uphill there, I mean really steep, there by that low-level rock we call the Table, and there's a seep. I got drinking water there. I was carrying that old tent bag with straps I'd found after some white boys had been camping on reservation land, drinking beer and howling at the moon, and had my water in that old thermos Grandmother liked.

"A red-tailed hawk passed over the ridge, her shadow crossing me and shooting down the ravine. I watched it disappear beyond a ridge and kept on walking, climbing higher, not going by Mercy Cleary's cabin, but going well above it. You know that dirt bluff clear of pine trees, just off the trail, with a view of the valley below and the ridges beyond, toward the *Urapitan* and the Kettle?

"I knew that Mercy Cleary wasn't home because there was fresh cornmeal along the head of that trail that comes up from behind her house, the way she does to protect her house when she's not home. I knew right where the archeologist was going. White men are pretty much predictable, you can tell what they're thinking by knowing what they want.

"I didn't go all the way to the top of Old Man's Back. I took that side trail, you know the one Sammy Greys covers with pine boughs, dry brown needles still on them, crisscrossing the mouth of the trail, so it won't feel like anybody ever walks that way. I was walking one of the spines of Old Man's Back, and it wasn't too far before I began to be able to see the hump in the old man's back. I was walking up through those scrawny pines where the rock is crumbly, and into that flat clearing where you can see all the way up Old Man's Back.

"It was hot out in the clearing, so I stood underneath the bough of a scrawny pine tree, and after awhile sat down on that rock like a box where the red squirrel like to strip those pine cones from the table-top pine. I watched the mountain be itself. The sky entered into that quiet when you're one with the world. And then I heard what I was looking for, the sound of metal, a pick ax striking rock. People shouldn't dig into the Earth, particularly with steel tools or machines.

"I looked over the edge of the cliff and down below me was that archeologist. I was out of his thoughts. His head was down and he was already digging angrily into the cliff face with a shovel. That anger was buried deep in him. The shovel head went back fast, glinting in the sun, and he cut with a sideways slash. I was close enough to hear the tumbling dirt and stone, a lonely grainy sound, but it looked like if he kept it up for very long he might give himself a heart attack. He was working too fast. He was a red-faced man, who only stopped to wipe the sweat out of his eyes and look at a piece of paper, a map that I'd say Knud Guunegai probably gave him. I looked around for Knud Guunegai, thinking maybe I'd see him, but all I saw were his crows. They came and perched in the tops of some of the tabletop pines and watched this white man too.

"I wasn't doing what I was doing for the Tribal Council. I was doing it for the Bear Clan. Where that archeologist was digging was sacred ground, and I could tell when he found the jaw of a dinosaur or something in the rock cliff. I started firing shots, about five seconds apart. I wasn't shooting at the archeologist; I was shooting around him. The bullets were hitting all around the rock and dirt where that white man was digging out that jawbone, and he seemed to know exactly what I was trying to do—

trying to scare him, but knowing I wasn't really going to shoot him. I knew that if I was going to scare that white man off I was going to have to land a bullet close enough to give him the idea that if I burped, a bullet might kill him.

"I'll say this for that archeologist: he was a brave man. I could have put those bullets as close as I wanted, could have put them in that Kowache's chest. But that white man got that jawbone out of the dirt while I was landing shots all around him. Most people would have run.

"The Tribal Council found out about it, and I guess it looked pretty bad, because the white man didn't have a gun, just a pick ax and a shovel. They felt they had to do something because, if they didn't, that archeologist might go report it to the county or state police or something, and there'd be some bad trouble for the tribe. The Tribal Council called me in and said they could drum me out of the tribe for doing what I did, and if I did it again that's what they'd do."

That was the story he told me.

That day Grandfather and me walked down the mountain, following the tire tracks of some white men who had come to the top of the mountain looking for something. They're always looking for something. We found where they had changed the oil in their truck, because they left empty oil cans, and there was a charred spot where they had burned the ground. I guess it was by accident because we couldn't see why they'd done that; there didn't seem to be any real reason for it.

"White men are stupid," Grandfather had said.

I thought he meant that they were unfeeling.

"No, they are men without spirits," Grandfather said. "I wouldn't come back here for awhile if I were you, Warren; this place is haunted."

What Grandfather meant when he said that had to do with why he called some white men ghosts, because if the body wasn't occupied by a spirit then the spirit had to be off somewhere else. This was almost unknown until the Kowache came. He said they had emotions they'd never paid attention to—anger and grief, fear, even guilt they didn't recognize—and that these emotions could prevent the spirit from coming back into the body if it had been travelling at night, as spirits will sometimes do when we are sleeping.

On the way down the mountain Grandfather tried to draw Death out from where Death was hiding by swearing at a white colonel he saw when we walked past a dirt road, coming up from the other side of the mountain, where this white colonel was talking with some of his men. They all had pistols in their belts. Grandfather called that colonel Monty Hall, what was a great insult in Grandfather's mind.

"Did that white colonel hear you?" I asked him.

"He's a ghost," Grandfather said. "He comes from the other world to mock me."

We walked until we came to a fork in the road,

except one of the roads leading up from the river was not used anymore and was overgrown with grass. When I was a kid it was a sandy road and we walked that way sometimes. It went by the Ghost Fields, but people stopped going that way. It was the road that came up from what was the village and had been made by the lives of many people. The new road, Reservation Road, came in from the west, and had been made by machines, bulldozers and graders.

Grandfather picked up a stick and began beating the bushes with it. He called out words I didn't understand. They were old words. He was wading into the blackberry bushes and thwacking the brambles and calling loudly for a spirit to come out.

"You can't fool me!" Grandfather called. I couldn't see anybody there. "I remember that you're here. There's no use hiding. I'm going to stay here until you come out or I'll never get on to dying today. Yah! Get out of there. Let me look at you!"

"What are you doing, Grandfather?" I said. "There's no one here."

But I knew that was a silly thing I said as soon as I said it. Grandfather either didn't hear me or didn't pay any attention to what I said, and he kept beating the blackberry bushes until a quail came flying out.

"You won't get away!" Grandfather called after the flying bird as it flew low into the woods where the old road led further down the mountain. "Hiding's no good. We'll find you!"

"What was that about?" I asked him.

"Death must be meaningful," Grandfather said. "I know that was one of them, one of those spirits who will trick you and get you to throw your life away as if it were a tin can."

And he set out walking. I didn't want to argue with Grandfather, but he was in a different world that day, or half in this one and half in the next one.

"But you've told me more than once that there is nothing useless," I finally said. "How can a life be useless?"

Grandfather laughed and stopped walking. Grandfather never talked while he walked. If Grandfather wanted to say something, or if I asked something, Grandfather would stop walking and turn around. "I didn't say a life could be useless. I said a death could be."

We went on silently except for the rhythm of the grasses swishing on our legs. The quail called loudly from the forest, and the song sparrow from a wild cherry tree, as we made our way down the mountain.

We came to a young woman, in a blue dress. I recognized the kind of dress as the old style. It wasn't the kind of thing you could buy in the store, and not many younger women wore them. I thought it must be the woman's mother's dress, some kind of a hand-me-down. I didn't recognize her anyway. She was picking blackberries and putting them in a basket.

No one spoke, though Grandfather was looking closely at the figure of the young woman, a smile on his face, like he wanted to touch her. She didn't turn away her gaze as young women often do when you gaze at them that way. She looked at the old man with open eyes. She'd stopped picking berries and seemed to be waiting for some word from us. I was taken by her beauty, but with Grandfather there, I wasn't comfortable with that, or with the silence. It's impolite not to address a young woman while taking in her beauty.

"Grandfather," I whispered, but he stood still as if he was charmed. Grandfather was next to helpless, and I knew he was something of a lech.

"Excuse me, but good afternoon... or good evening," I began in Grandfather's stead, for it's unusual for the young to speak before the old in such a situation. Old men are usually better at putting young women at ease anyway.

"Where are you going?" the young woman said. I could not keep my eyes off her breasts. They were luscious and wet. She had been sweating in her dress, and the moist blue cotton clung to her hips. Her eyes were immeasurably dark. Her black hair was tied back revealing the length of her neck. I felt a surge in my loins coming on, so I spoke quickly to keep my blood from getting excited.

"We are going to the old village, I think," I said.

A horsefly flew around the young woman's head several times. I thought to help her for I knew just what to do with horseflies. But the young woman let the horsefly land on her calf, looking down at it almost tenderly, and then snatched it up with her free hand. When she cupped it in her hand I wondered if she was going to crush it the way most of our people did. Instead, she shook it fiercely in her open fist, and with several words of warning to the horsefly, threw it into the air. It was just as Grandfather had taught me to do, catch a horsefly, how to shake and rattle them inside your hand, telling them not to come back or you might have to kill them.

"Do our people always do this with horseflies?" I had asked him once. I had never seen anyone else in the tribe doing such a thing with horseflies.

"No, I do this," Grandfather had said.

By the time I came back from my remembering the young woman had vanished, as if she had never been there at all.

"What happened, Grandfather? Who was that?"

"We won't meet any white men along this road. They are behind us now," Grandfather said.

"But there was a young woman here. She was beautiful," I said.

"She was not for you, and yet you saw her. That's good," Grandfather said. "She was your grand-mother."

I was thunderstruck, and there was a moment when I felt helpless, like I was supposed to know the rules of two different worlds, and live in them both at the same time. I couldn't do it.

"What are we doing?" I asked.

"It's the old way," Grandfather said. "White men teach what they believe, but now you are seeing the way it can't be done with talk. Now let's get going; I have some dying to do."

We left the grass and the thickets and went down inside the moist forest, where the sound of the wind sometimes comes and goes through the tops of the rock maples and the chestnut oaks. The stones were grown with moss, and here, on other days, we had gathered black rattlesnake root for Aunt Ida. The sun was low in the sky.

In the silence the darkness deepened in the lateness of the day, and I couldn't help but wonder what I would do if Grandfather died down there by the old village on the river. I found myself thinking of a plan of how and when I would tell Aunt Ida, and then go find Ruby so they could walk down the mountain with flashlights. I was wondering about this when a vesper thrush flew across the trail, a dark form in the growing shadows.

"Let's go walking in Mr. Brown's cornfield," Grandfather said.

I remembered a day years before and Grandfather leading me into that same cornfield. He had spread his arms and whirled them around, kicking corn stalks violently, in a straight path toward the river.

"Mr. Brown will think Brother Bear did it," Grandfather had said.

Now Grandfather simply walked into the cornfield, his arms by his sides. The sun was fading into a softer glow and the moon began its rise above the tree line, mostly maples bordering the river, quiet now by the cornfield. "You don't want to ever surprise a bear in a cornfield," I remembered Grandfather had said.

We walked to the middle of the cornfield. Grandfather and I stood together somewhere down there in the middle of the cornfield, watching the moon come up. Then Grandfather quietly took his clothes off. I watched him, wondering if I should take my clothes off. When Grandfather dropped his pants and walked out of them toward the river, I followed him. I took my clothes off, hearing Grandfather singing some old song as he walked off. He was trying to knock the corn down, slinging his weak old arms around him as if they didn't quite belong to him. Most of the corn was still half-standing until I came along after him, and out of respect, kicked it down and stepped on it.

Grandfather sat down on a big old tree root down by the river where it pooled, darkly moving in the unknown. I could feel Grandfather sinking into one of those bouts of silence, what I had known in him from time to time after Grandmother died.

"What are you going to do, Grandfather?" I asked.

"I'm going to wait here until Death comes for me," he said. "Death is always hiding, but sometimes, if you wait in the woods alone, you can hear Death creeping up from behind, and if you can keep yourself from looking, Death will come right up behind you and look over your shoulder. But if you try to look, it's no good. Death will run away and you'll be afraid, way down deep inside where you can pretend you don't know it."

I realized then that Grandfather was allowing me, inviting me, to witness his death. It was the old way, something we Uwharrie had once done.

I reached down in the dark and found a pebble. I fingered it awhile there in the dark, tempted by something stirring inside me to throw it into the water the way a white man would, but I caught myself. I recognized my own fear. I named it.

Grandfather hadn't moved. The water flowed and we sat there together on that big root of the tree down by the dark river.

"Who we are is not the white man's fault," Grandfather said, "though he is caught up in illusions and the power there is to create them. We thought, 'Maybe the white man is right.' We listened to his arguments, and we seemed powerless against them. But I remember how it was, how we were quiet inside, and didn't think of what to say before it was time to say it. We did all things by waiting. Time was the river. We made our village on its banks. We bathed in it and drank its waters. We sat here beside it and our thoughts were right."

I was listening to Grandfather, and listening to the soft sound of water below, the ripples of darkness, everything floating away downstream. It was peaceful down by the river. It always has been.

After that, the world was a lonelier place.

Aunt Ida helped Ruby and me prepare the body. Aunt Ida and Ruby wouldn't let me leave Grandfather in the cornfield like I wanted to, but we built a frame of ash back up in the woods, where the white men couldn't know about it, and laid him on top so the crows could make his body return to the great circle of the universe. Afterwards I cut down a maple tree and sawed out a big section of trunk. I set it up on two tall stones so the sap could flow out both ways, so Grandfather's spirit could settle any unfinished business he had in this world. That is traditional.

Almost a year after Sun Susie disappeared, her coat turned up down at Gannon's Motel. It had been found in one of the motel rooms by a cleaning lady who'd found it one morning after some man staying in that room had checked out. The cleaning lady had just put a tag on it saying which room it was found in the day she found it and stuck it in a closet used for lost and found items. One day they decided to clean out the closet, and one of the cleaning ladies asked about selling all that stuff, so one Saturday morning they hauled all that stuff out of the closet—shoes, shirts, pants, coats, hats, umbrellas, books—and had a garage sale in the parking lot. There were cans of food, hair dryers, irons, hot plates, a couple of toasters. There was even a pair of deer antlers, and a guitar, and there was Sun Susie's coat. Beja Locklear was the one who recognized it.

The motel had the name of the man who had stayed in the room where the coat was found, and an address, but that was about all because the man had paid in cash. They didn't remember him anyway. He had only stayed a couple of nights, and that was the week before Sun Susie disappeared.

That's what got people talking, and Indians can make up stuff better than anybody. Sun Susie's name didn't show up anywhere on the motel register. That didn't mean she didn't stay there though, and a lot of people thought she had stayed with that man those several nights he was in the motel.

Ruby said maybe something like that could happen, but she didn't think it did, and I didn't either. We pretty much figured if you could find out who this guy was you'd find out who killed Sun Susie.

The man in the motel room was from Los Angeles, but his name turned out to be a dead end. The police looked into it: there wasn't any such address in Los Angeles, and he'd given a phony name. Then everybody thought this man *had* probably killed Sun Susie but that there would be no way to find him.

You could fill a *National Enquirer* with the stories being told down at the Legion Hall about this man from Los Angeles. It was better than a magazine. I'd hear everything, from that the man was a carnie looking for an Indian's skin to put into a pickle jar, to the man was an FBI agent investigating Sun Susie's disappearance.

"Well, there's more than a few who've died mysteriously and a couple that ain't been found," Gettis Strange said. "There was June Goins down that dirt road off Highway 10. Cox Stevenson and Cousin Ben Colin Long. They didn't just up and move off the Reservation, and none of their relatives know where they are. There was Knud Guunegai too. Shit, he didn't die of exposure."

"Hell, Cousin Ben Colin Long didn't disappear," Lester Keestrong said. "He joined the army."

"Who told you that? Cousin Ben Colin Long

never joined the army. Why's he going to join the army?" Gettis said.

"Indians disappear because they know too much," Thomas Matoas Paint said.

"Hell, Thomas," Gettis said, "Sun Susie didn't know shit. She isn't dead at all. She didn't disappear; she ran off with that man from Los Angeles. I bet she's living in Los Angeles today. I think she's got family out there."

"Then the man *was* an FBI agent," Lees Kramer said.

"You can think she's alive if you like to. It doesn't make any difference to her what you think," Thomas said. "But Ruby, Warren's sister, she pretty much figured it out first, and I think she's right." Everybody looked at me.

Ruby didn't come to the Legion Hall much anymore, and never to play pool; the Presbyterians had gotten to her. She'd remarried, a guy named Si Fishback, and he was big into the Bible and the revivals. Used to be we'd come down to the Legion Hall and Ruby'd stick Anthony John on his cradleboard against the wall so he could watch the pool balls and their moving colors. He'd laughed at the clacking sound the pool balls made when they smacked together.

Thomas took a swig off his beer. "You guys ain't figured it out yet? Sun Susie didn't either, but still, she died for it. Warren, you tell them. She's your sister."

He said that because Thomas knew that I knew

better than anyone, blood to blood, how Ruby'd done everything she could to find out what happened to Sun Susie. All that hard-headedness Ruby always had, she spent on trying to really understand what had happened. It meant everything to her. I don't know exactly why. But even so, there were still things we would never know.

"Sun Susie was pulling records at the hospital," I said, "and she knew Margaret Brown couldn't have died of diabetes. Margaret Brown didn't have diabetes that bad. Thomas here knew that. Margaret couldn't have had the insulin levels they say she had. Her problem was she trusted a doctor, and it was more than a little bit suspicious that Sam Brown, her son, died within two weeks of his mother, way off somewhere by himself."

"What are you saying, Warren?" Gettis asked.

But Thomas jumped in then. He was just plain too excited. I could see Thomas's blue eyes flashing to a light inside, what the truth did to him. It could be the nature of the universe, or something in the details, like when a good person died for the wrong reason.

"Margaret Brown was a traditional. She kept the old ways. I was treating her for diabetes. Warren, you know how I do that. She wasn't that sick. But you know all that allotment stuff, she never went in for that. When they came to her and said she owned the land, and that if she signed a little piece of paper she could get money for it, she didn't do it. She told them she couldn't sign a paper like she owned the land. The land owned her. They couldn't understand what she was talking about, and maybe she couldn't understand mineral rights, but she knew enough not to sign her land away. Maybe Sam knew what their business was about. But do you know what happened to her land after she died?"

Thomas waited. He wanted to be sure we were all listening. A glint in his blue eyes flashed around the room, catching everyone's attention.

"It went back to the tribe, and the Tribal Council decided what happened with that land, both hers and her son's, after he died. The tribe voted to lease that land out for mineral rights, along with Knud Guunegai's, more than 900 acres of land. They leased it to the U.S. Petroleum Corporation, along with Bejjie Rose's land, Corlay Hathale's land, and Hahay Charlie's.

"But they ain't ever gonna put a face to that crime. Some man does it but it's really the corporation that gets him to do the dirty work. Union Carbide, Ford Motor Company, U.S. Petroleum, the U.S. government—they're all corporations and they're all about the money they'll make, all the rights of a man without the conscience of one."

They did find the man from Los Angeles; it just wasn't the way they thought they would. In the early nineties the Tribal Council gave permission for some archeologists to go up around Old Man's Back, and the archeologists had to pay Carl Youngblood to go up there with them, kind of like a tribal watchdog to make sure they dug where they said they were going to dig. It was a good job. Carl'd sit around in the shade all day and read Tony Hillerman novels, and every once in awhile they'd call for him to check and see what they'd found. The agreement was if the Tribal Council didn't like what they had taken from the ground, those archeologists would have to put it back. That's what they did when they found human bones. Whenever they found something important Carl would watch them put a tag on it, and he'd nod his head and go back to reading in the shade.

Carl Youngblood had a black lab named Oprah. Oprah was a wandering dog. She didn't like just sitting around all day. She'd wait around to see if Carl was going to do anything that day, and if he wasn't she'd take herself for a walk. She'd be gone for hours. Oprah went everywhere with Carl, go to the grocery store, go to the Legion Hall, go the movies, ride beside him in his old blue Valiant. And Oprah went with him to that dig site. Carl said she wouldn't stick around long and would take herself up into the hills to chase deer and kill lizards and snakes.

She brought back deer legs, shoulder bones, deer hooves, toad skins, any old part of some carcass she found, but one day she comes trotting back to the dig site carrying a skull in her mouth. At first everybody just thought it was a deer skull and let her chew on that skull, sitting over underneath a tree and just chomping on that skull until it was time to go. Carl said he wasn't going to let her take that skull back in his car and he took the skull away from her. But it wasn't a deer skull at all; it was a human skull. They started looking around to see if they could find anything else. They didn't, but the next day they closed that dig site down, and there were cop cars all over the place. They found a shoulder bone and an arm bone, and not in the same place, because I guess animals carried those bones around. I thought it was going to be Sun Susie because that's where I figured that white guy had buried her.

They looked all that day and some of the next day, and they found more of a skeleton. It turned out it was a man. They guessed that from the length of the arm bone and some other bones. Coyotes and mountains lions had spread him all over the place, and mice had even carried off some of the smaller bones. They found a knuckle bone in a tree.

At first they didn't know who it was. I don't know if they ever found all of him. Mostly people thought it was Cox Stevenson or Cousin Ben Colin Long. It was ten years before they found out who it was. Back in the nineties they couldn't tell who a pile of bones was, but they kept all those bones, and a couple of years ago they did DNA testing, on the teeth, those bones, and some bits of hair they found chewed into the skull by what they thought was a bear or a mountain lion or something. I know it was a mountain lion.

The man was from Los Angeles, and his name was Andrew Parvel, a Mafia type, arrested for possession and running guns to Mexico. His big trick was killing people for money: check himself into a motel under a false name and then check himself out, but once he'd ended up getting shot, turned up in a hospital and became part of a DNA database.

The police never did determine a cause of death for Andrew Parvel, and didn't know what he was doing over behind Old Man's Back, but Thomas Matoas Paint, Ruby and me, we knew. We knew Sun Susie was buried somewhere behind Old Man's Back, and they were probably never going to find her. We never knew where the money had come from exactly, but we knew big business was in on it, and Ruby figured out how Joe had got saved from Vietnam by getting caught up in that whole mess, and he didn't even know it. She never told him who pulled out on him that day on his motorcycle. I finally did, but only that it was the same white guy who had probably killed Sun Susie. I just left it to him to figure out whatever he had to figure out, just like how I had to figure out about Mercy Cleary, how she'd been watching out for us all that time, and then her time was gone. It was time for me to live in my power, which is different than what a white man means by that; responsibility is no more than the ability to respond to any situation. Everything's a story, and we're part of it. I didn't know how the stories connected us, the stories of who we are and why things are.

I go to see Joseph Calaitl sometimes. He's the last. I hadn't known Joseph Calaitl but as a big fat Indian with diabetes who lived by himself. At one time I couldn't understand how Joseph Calaitl could be happy despite all of his afflictions: diabetes, swollen legs and feet, cuts that wouldn't heal and bruises that never seemed to go away, and everybody had forgotten him. At one time he was a leader among us, but there weren't many of the young who knew him really. He was by himself so much.

He had a big family though, and they came and visited him, cut wood, bought groceries, pulled the stockings off his swollen feet every day. He lived in a grey cinder-block house with aluminum windows. There were a lot of those on the Reservation. He had an old black dog that lived there with him, an old friendly dog with emphysema, who barked like a husky smoker's cough and struggled to get up, like an old man, when I came to the door. That dog went right back to sleep once Joseph Calaitl got up out of his easy chair to see who I was. I think he kind of wondered why I came to see him.

I would offer to help with fixing the tea he made for us, but he wouldn't have any of that. He was fiercely independent and, though he must've weighed more than three hundred pounds and was old, he wanted to do as much as he could by himself. I had never had any tea like what Joseph Calaitl drank. It was black like coffee but it tasted like tannin, like soaked acorns.

"What is it?"

"Holly. I didn't sleep too good last night," Joseph
Calaitl said. I learned pretty soon that Joseph Calaitl
didn't talk about things that were happening in the
present time very much, except having to do with
how he had slept the last night, or how his feet hurt,
or the last time he had fallen.

The first thing we talked about that first time I
went to see him was how he had ended up in the
Presbyterian Hospital about a month before because
he collapsed one morning on the way to the bathroom. He told me about it in detail, like it had happened yesterday: what he was thinking lying there on
the floor and not able to get up; how it didn't hurt so
much as he thought it would, but he thought he was
going to die; how he had seemed very much at peace
with it; and how Homey, that was the name of that
old black dog of his, had come and licked him in the
face. Joseph Calaitl was struck by the fact that Homey
knew there was something wrong with him, but that
dog couldn't do anything either. Sometime later his
daughter had come in and his son-in-law, or she had
called him. Joseph Calaitl wasn't sure, and he told a
confused story about the paramedics coming and
putting him on a stretcher, and how he joked with
them about how they wouldn't be able to carry him.
He told me that joke three times. I knew he remembered he had; he just liked that joke.

We drank that bitter tea and he told me about the
hospital, about the young doctor and the needles they

put in him, and a long story about how they were going to release him one day and then they didn't because they didn't like what his insulin was doing. I asked him if it was Dr. Stevenson.

He looked at me out of both eyes, the way Grandfather used to do. He could turn you to smoke with the clarity of his gaze.

"You know I'm diabetic," he said.

"Yeah, I think I knew that," I said.

Joseph Calaitl laughed. "I wouldn't let that son of a bitch work on me."

I had another cup of tea, and before I knew it, a few hours had gone by. It was getting dark outside and I said I had to go, which seemed to surprise him, or disappoint him, like we were just getting started. I guess, in a kind of way, we were, because we hadn't talked about much of anything except how he had fallen on the floor and how his daughter had found him and what the hospital was like, how they didn't seem to know what they were doing.

"Well, you'll just have to come back," he said. And between his easy chair and the door he told me, "There's nothing on this Reservation that's not a story where something happened. Sometimes it's not the exact date when that thing happened that's important, but the place or location where it happened, and someone was there to see it. That's life, and that life got passed on in a story. The life is each of us. It might be long, long ago, or not so long ago. It might be Christmas Creek where the ferns have been growing on the hillside leading down to the river since no one remembers when, or Malaika's Bald, because the Great One sent down lightning, setting fire to the top of the mountain where a giant lived who was eating the children, and the people went up and saw his charred bones. You should come back."

I'd been there three hours and he told me more in a half-minute than I knew my whole life. That old dog Homey didn't even get up.

Of course I did go back, and the next time I went there I found things I hadn't known that I knew. It was the beginning of something and the end of something.

Before I could sit down he said, "Would you like some gin?"

"Gin?" I said.

"Yes, would you like some gin? That's what I'm asking you."

"I didn't know you drank gin."

"My daughters don't want me to, because I'm diabetic. But I do it, and you can't tell them. Would you like some gin?"

Well, I could tell that Joseph wanted some gin. I didn't drink gin, but I drank gin with Joseph Calaitl. The gin was good. It didn't taste good but it felt good, and it warmed the brain and loosened the tongue, and in some strange way it sharpened the mind, and pretty soon we were talking about Old Man's Back. Joseph Calaitl started telling stories he thought he'd forgotten. I learned from him that there was a lot of truth behind the words that Chief Billy had helped maintain our self-government when the U.S. government was threatening not to renegotiate our sovereignty.

"Are you sure?"

"Yeah, I'm sure. There's no judgment on the inside. I'm not saying Chief Billy always had the well-being of the tribe in mind, but sometimes he did. They never went looking for oil or uranium or any-thing up behind Old Man's Back. Oh yeah, he'd let an archeologist go up there to keep the white people happy. That land is Uwharrie. It will always be Uwharrie."

He hadn't been up on Old Man's Back in twenty years, because he'd gotten so fat and could hardly walk, but he remembered the land up there better than I could.

"I've walked all over that mountain," he said. "Did your grandfather ever say anything bad about Chief Billy?"

"Well, yeah, he did."

Joseph Calaitl got that mischievous look in his eye, like when he's amused. "Yeah, I guess I can see he would have, but did your Grandfather ever tell you how I used to go up there and steal their shovels, the keys to their trucks, let the air out of their tires? You wouldn't know it now by looking at me, but I could walk all over that mountain."

"Yeah, he said something about that. He went up there too, right?"

"Yes, I guess he did. Did he ever tell you any stories?"

"He told me one about shooting at an archeologist who was digging out a dinosaur jawbone."

"Did he now? And have you gone up there?"

"What do you mean?"

"Have you gone to where that was? Your grandfather told you a story, and now you're telling me, so it must be an important story. Have you been up there where he shot at that archeologist?"

"No."

"Well, you need to go up there. You need to go see that place. If your grandfather told you that story, I guess you know how to get there."

"Yes, I know the way."

I followed the words of the story, went that way again that Grandfather had told me. I took water with me in a plastic Coke bottle, took that old compression sack Grandfather had found that the white boys left him, and walked up the old logging road up there on Old Man's Back. Somebody was still laying brush on that side path, and I walked out on the spine through the scrawny pines to that clearing, and stood at the cliff's edge.

I heard the *skrrrrr!* of that red-tailed hawk. The shadow passed over me and I looked up and saw her. She was looking down at me, and I could see myself standing there at the cliff's edge, and I knew in my mind just how Old Man's Back looked with the spurs coming off a backbone, and how the mountain could look like the spinal column of an old drying-up man. It wasn't words; it was an image I saw in my mind's eye. She passed over me and sailed across the next bony ridge, watching for ground squirrels and rabbits' mistakes.

I climbed down along the cliff to the place I remembered in words, where the white man had been digging with his shovel. I saw the notches in the rock where a couple of Grandfather's bullets struck the rock. Grandfather taught me how to shoot a .22 rifle when I was seven years old, and took me and Joe Bad Crow hunting with him when I was eight. I killed my first deer when I was twelve. I had forgotten I knew how Grandfather had taught us to shoot, how he painted a black circle on an old white shirt and hung that old shirt on the clothesline, and he told us to hit the shirt as many times as we could in ten shots, without hitting the black circle. I remembered that and put my finger into one of the bullet notches in the rock, and there was rock powder there like it was yesterday.

Just then I heard the song of a wren and I looked, and there, perched on an old hemlock which had fallen across the gulch, was a brown wren, and he hopped down into a kind of hollow in the rock not more than forty feet from me. I watched him from the silence behind seeing, the endless moment where there is no thinking, and I knew there was something there. I didn't know how I knew it, but it was at the end of my gaze that I would find it. Out of respect for the little wren, I waited, in the breathless breathing of knowing. I don't know how long it was before the wren flew away and I went to the hollow of the rock to see what was there.

I knew what it was when I saw it, because of that day Chief Billy had those U.S. geologists or whoever they were showing up for those samples of uranium. I hadn't remembered how much I knew until I saw it. Some of that rock up in the gulch was almost red, like rusting iron, and they had talked about that, how sometimes uranium veins were embedded in that kind of rock. These were almost a foot apart, but the veins were dark, just like the ore they'd shown us. I knew that's what it was. Even without the description those men gave us, I knew what it was. I don't remember the name of the kind of rock the uranium ore was embedded in, but there it was, pitchblende or uranite.

I took a piece of quartz—there was plenty of that up there—and I scratched at the rock in the vein, and it came off black, just like they said it did.

Sometimes things aren't what they seem, and it dawned on me then—it had to—that Chief Billy might not have been as bad as I thought he was. Maybe he was no Grey Legs, maybe he used tribal funds to get himself a new truck, build an addition on his house, but maybe he kept the U.S. out of our sacred grounds by letting them dig up a few dinosaur bones. I don't know. It seems that way to me now, that maybe that's what he was doing. Politics is a funny thing, whether it's Indian, Chinese or a white man's. It's possible that that's what he was really doing.

Chief Billy died of a heart attack, probably a result of cardiovascular disease. He was sixty-four years old, died of a heart attack. Maybe it was because he smoked cigarettes, but he ate a lot of bacon grease, butter and eggs too. He had some bad arthritis pain so he didn't get too much exercise. Still he wasn't fat, not like Joseph Calaitl, and he's still alive and as big as a house.

Most people these days aren't happy the way they are, and I don't mean just white people. It's Indians too. Once we were pretty much happy with the ways things were. Everything: living and dying, being old or being young, being a woman or a man, having three legs if that's the way you're born. But now there's a lot of people who think the rock they're sitting on would look better if it was resting on top of a mountain.

But I have begun living my name, the Seed. I am keeping the stories. Many of the old ways are lost. It is a new day. Joseph Calaitl told me many things, but he said that Mercy Cleary was right: no one would be able to speak the old language when she was gone, that what I would know, what anyone would know, would never again be truly Uwharrie. It would be something else. Maybe it's the church, maybe it's school, but it's not the head which makes an authentic human being. It isn't even being Indian that makes anybody authentic. I'd say now there are Indians who are not authentic human beings. Oh, they say they're Indian alright; they've got their Indian card. "I'm a card-carrying Indian." But that's just one more brand of assimilation. Like reservation schools, churches and bibles, just another way to that endless feeling of not being worthy. Communities fall apart and people feel unworthy.

There were fifty or sixty years where the traditional ways were not practiced openly. Fifty or sixty years when not many were going up on the Mountain. Most people were just trying to figure out how to live the white man's way because that was the way to survive. "There ain't no future in the old ways." I heard that plenty of times when I was growing up. Somebody'd be buying a can of condensed milk and they'd say, "Ain't no future in the old ways."

Uwharries don't have a word for time. A better word for time is story. It's all story. All moments that ever were, are in one place. But the Reservation is a concept. The white man invented it, a system of thought, a manifestation of his mind. He said to us, "We are going to put you inside our concept. You are going to live there." The white man drew the lines.

I don't know how I fully know it, but living Uwharrie means to belong, and this is something which is practiced every day. It is when we say "hello" and "Isn't it a beautiful day?" because the words coming back to us from our brothers and our sisters verify that we are sharing experience, that life is shared. We are a people, as individuals with responsibilities, as members of a clan with responsibilities to others, and as Uwharrie responsible to all life.

The seed of consciousness is planted in childhood. This consciousness is not our bodies; it is not our minds. True living is loving: this land, the Earth, the people we share life with. The highways, the lines of automobiles, the power lines, the business of cities and states, these are all illusions, the appearance of life. A man can just *think* he's living. It's an illusion, only he doesn't know it. Everything has the seed of consciousness planted inside of it: the oak tree, the hawk, the grasshopper, the moth, the trout. They all have a consciousness. Ultimately, this consciousness doesn't separate us, it connects us.

The seed of consciousness is not an Indian thing. One day you think you're one person, and the next day you're another. You say, "This is who I am," and the next thing you know you're somebody else. We are connected this way. This is what it is to be reborn in this lifetime.

You are walking down the street and you see a man with no arm, got it chewed up in a sawmill. You want to look at that? Not really. But do you want to look at yourself? He doesn't want to look at himself, but sooner or later, he's got to or it'll take a hold of him and never let him go. Man wheeling himself down the street in a wheelchair, got a sign, says "Vietnam Vet." He's got no legs. You want to look at that? Does he want to look at that? Maybe not, but it's much worse to be crippled inside. My medicine power is the owl. I can see what others don't know about themselves and I can see when they're sick because of it. Got a swollen knee, addicted to cocaine, coffee, cigarettes, power, whatever. There's nothing wrong with them, but they might want to give up smoking three packs of cigarettes a day, or maybe stop being so mad at their father and forgive him because he's dead.

I don't how people got started thinking that what they thought didn't affect their bodies or affect anything else.

This is why white people are so sick. They think

everything is outside of them, separate. "Why am I subject to the sun? Why do I have to be so hot? Why do I have to be so cold? Why am I subject to the Earth and moon? And to the rain? I don't want to be wet. Why is there disease and why do I have to get old and die?" This is the biggest problem with white people.

It is not true that we come here only to live; there is another world of which most people are only dimly, if ever, aware. The Kowache would probably call it invisible because they can only imagine that it is here. But the truth includes the living *and* the dead. The only moment that exists is this moment, but in this moment is the story of everything. Everything is here. This truth of which I speak is not impermanent. It runs through the motion of the rivers and the oceans; it runs through the veins of our body, these bones of our existence. It sounds itself in the wind, and comes in the voice of the rain. The ways of the Kowache will pass, their influence will fade like the waning moon, because they are founded upon lies.